DRAGON MAGE

Dragon Point Seven

EVE LANGLAIS

Copyright © 2020/2021, Eve Langlais

Cover Art by Yocla Designs © 2020/2021

Produced in Canada

Published by Eve Langlais

http://www.EveLanglais.com

Digital ISBN: 978 177384 160 1

Print ISBN: 978 177384 161 8

Prologue

The end of the world began its steady march because of a cat. No one was surprised.

S omewhere in an arid land, where the sun beat down, baking the dirt, at the very rear of a shelf, in a closet rarely opened, sat a bottle that never gathered any dust. More than a century now it had occupied that spot. And before that, ten times as long in another home, showcased with pride. An heirloom passed down along the generations, so many of them that the story of the glass amphora was lost, its true value forgotten. Thus the bottle was hidden away and ignored.

The amphora bided its time. Settled quietly on that shelf, unassuming, waiting. Over the years, the muffled voices and noises that penetrated its hiding spot changed, as did the bedding shoved into this rarely used closet, each new sheet and pillowcase pushing the container farther back until it found itself in the farthest corner, never even sensing daylight.

It waited some more.

One day, something exploded nearby—it could have been a bomb or even a gas stove—rattling the very structure of the house, shifting the old stone. The bottle wobbled for a second, but cushioned between the wall and bedding, it steadied.

The house remained standing. For now.

But the process had begun. A crack appeared. Then another.

No one repaired the damage. And it got worse. A bullet came right through a window, the angle just right to hit the wooden closet door, where it remained wedged. Not close enough to help, but apparently enough to empty the house.

It didn't remain abandoned for long. Transients moved in, searching the place top to bottom, looking for anything of value. They rummaged in the closet, shoving in their arms, their hands never quite reaching deep enough past the musty sheets to find the bottle.

The closet slammed shut, and the amphora quivered. Close. So close.

It wasn't long before they returned, yanking on

the sheets and blankets stuffed in the closet. They pulled out everything they could, revealing the bottle.

The glass was dragged forward enough to be seen. Daylight at last.

Freedom was at hand.

Open me.

Rather than crack the top, the less-than-gentle hands shook the amphora. Peered at it. It almost got tossed to the ground.

Do it.

The bottle was placed back in the closet, intact. The vagrants left, but they didn't close the door.

Soon a new occupant moved in, a feline with ribs showing through its fur and a crooked-tipped tail. It sauntered past the closet, teasing with its leisurely walk.

Come here.

The cat didn't even deign to look. It left.

But it returned the next day. It entered the closet, drawn by a bobbing pinpoint of light refracted from the bottle. The cat chased it around, almost knocking over the amphora. It came close a few times, but the feline proved too graceful, teasing the amphora instead with the silken rub of its fur. As if to taunt, it spent the night curled around the bottle.

It took several days before the feline finally

tipped it over and rolled the glass close enough to the edge. The tip of it protruded over the shelf. So close to falling.

Just give it a tiny push.

Because cats were ornery, it pushed the bottle away from the edge to the back of the shelf.

The bottle waited some more.

The feline skipped a few days before returning, this time playing more roughly with the bobbing pinpoint of light, knocking the glass hard enough it rolled to the edge.

Almost there…

The bottle didn't fall, but it wouldn't need much.

Here, kitty, kitty. Less actual words and more a thought. A command the cat ignored. It lay down and groomed itself.

Had to admire its suave nature. The bottle bounced a pinprick of light, trying to draw its attention. The cat chose to lick its genital area instead.

Apparently, today was not the day. Or maybe it would never happen. It should resign itself to spending eternity on the shelf.

The cat rolled and stretched, reaching out a paw that it placed on the bottle. Right on the spot. Only the slightest nudge would send it over the edge. The anticipation made the amphora hum with sound.

The feline growled and rolled to its feet. It hunched over the bottle.

Push me.

The cat hissed.

Hit me. The bottle glowed and hummed some more. The cat's growl rose in pitch, and it batted the threat.

The bottle tipped and dropped to the hard tile floor. It didn't so much shatter as splinter. Hairline cracks formed in the glass. The cat leaped down beside it and sniffed.

The impact lines spread, and a hum of sound escaped. A hint of something *other*. The cat cocked its head and leaned closer for a better sniff just as the bottle exploded.

The cat yowled and wished it were somewhere else.

An ancient scream was released as the prison disintegrated, setting events into motion.

Deep in a desert, the ground trembled as an ancient tomb opened. Fissures appeared in the hard-packed dirt, turning it back into sand, the fine grains and pebbles sinking into the earth. An entire section dropped away, showing a widening funnel that swirled, churning rock into sand and getting bigger, as if a stopper had been pulled, until it all ran out.

A rift that hadn't been accessed in three thousand years opened with a burst of power that radiated, pulsing outward, and all things living felt its passing. They just didn't understand what it meant.

The innocence before the storm.

From within the whirlpool of dirt appeared four shapes atop steeds made of bone. As they marched steadily upward, motes of sand and dust coalesced to give their mounts shape. Of those riding them, nothing could be seen but the cloaks that covered them. They trotted up the side of the funnel as if gravity did not apply. The heavy plods of the hooves made steady progress up the slope. They said not a word.

At the rim of the funnel, they each chose a direction to face. Everywhere they looked, they could see only a barren wasteland.

And a mangy cat.

It stood north of the rift and meowed. A hand, encased in a gauntlet, leaned down to grasp it. Set it on its saddle. The horsemen kicked their heels and set off. No need to discuss their plans. They'd had three thousand years to hone them, waiting for the day they'd return.

They shimmered from view, as if a mirage, and yet that didn't stop a dragoness named Elspeth—who sometimes saw things no one else did—from stirring in her sleep and muttering, "Should have known it would be a cat that broke the first of the seals."

That left six.

Six chances to keep a great evil out of the world. But first, they should probably deal with the horsemen of the apocalypse.

Chapter One

Her very pink T-shirt: I don't believe in ghosts.
I'm an archeologist.

The artifacts arrived in wooden crates, sealed tight and packed with popcorn foam that cushioned smaller solid boxes.

Daphne shoved her glasses up on her nose as she took a moment to stare. This was more exciting than Christmas, for her at least. Canada so rarely enjoyed such exciting archeological finds, and yet a ruin was found, by accident, in the depths of a lake in Northern Ontario. A beaver dam had caused the water supply to the lake to run dry. Dry enough that the ruins that hid at the very bottom became exposed. Steps, leading to a dais. A few toppled pillars. The stone pitted and eroded by water and time, yet clearly manmade. But which era? Who built them? That had yet to be determined. The few artifacts recovered had been catalogued and studied. Everyone was stumped, so while the historians and scientists scratched their befuddled heads, the amazing finds would go on display at the Canadian Museum of History.

Which was the most exciting thing ever!

The archeological find of the century and Daphne was in charge of setting it up.

First, though, precautions. She wore a clean white coat over her regular clothes. Her hair was tied back, and a surgical mask covered the bottom half of her face. Mostly to block smells. Old things didn't always have the most pleasant scents.

Giddy excitement filled her as she laid her gloved hands on the precious artifacts. She knew better than to leave any skin oils on them.

First out of the crate, wrapped in bubble, a chunk of stone about two inches thick, possibly the remnant of a stone tablet. The amazing part? The carvings in it. Weird symbols that reminded her of Egyptian glyphs and yet didn't match any currently on file. The linguists were creaming themselves in excitement over a new dead language.

She ran her fingers through the faint grooves. So awesome. Especially since one of the symbols reminded her of a dragon in flight. She loved dragons. She actually collected them. Only handmade ones: carved soapstone, blown glass, and several metal pieces of art. It never ceased to amaze her how the dragon showed up in so many different cultures around the world and going far back, too.

Some in her circle speculated that the dragons depicted in ancient texts were actually the remnants of dinosaurs. Flying reptiles that ended up going extinct.

Others were convinced dragons actually existed because of recent media footage of people claiming to have caught them.

Was it real? Hard to tell with today's excellent CGI, but what if it were true? What if dragons were real?

Maybe she could meet one up close. Pet it.

Keep it.

Okay, maybe she couldn't keep a dragon.

Unless…there were some people saying dragons could shapeshift to look like humans. Which she personally thought was physically impossible. Dragons were big. People were small. It just didn't work.

Unless the dragons were small.

Which would make it easier to keep one.

She forgot about dragons and concentrated on her job again, placing the stone chunk carefully on her trolley.

Next, she uncovered an old dagger, forged out of some unidentified metal. Not bronze or copper, it was something that they'd not yet been able to identify. The speculation was the metal was probably harvested from a meteor. But who did it belong to? There'd never been anything other than prehistoric tools found this far into the continent. This predated the first settlers.

Its discovery would change the history of the country! And she got to see it and touch it before the general public. Her hands shook a little as she placed the dagger onto her trolley, giving it a light stroke. Total nerdgirl-gasm.

Wrapped in layers of bubblewrap, she uncovered a vase comprised of pottery shards that had been glued together. They'd managed to recreate the pot, albeit with missing pieces. It took some delicate handling, as she feared it coming apart.

Only one box left. The one she'd intentionally kept for last because it fascinated her the most. Of all the things found in that lake, it proved the most controversial, firstly because it should have never survived. Glass, in a lake that had frozen and thawed countless times? The bottle should have long ago shattered, which led to arguments, as some claimed it wasn't part of the ruins. It must have sunk there more recently. But they shut up when all the tests they ran pegged it as being old. As in more than a thousand years old.

It had been located in a chamber accessed via a hidden doorway in the center of the dais. Apparently it was like something out of a movie, the way a certain stone, when shifted, caused it to rumble open. The room beneath was filled with water, and so divers were sent in. A team of three. Two of them had seizures and died before they could be pulled back up. The third retrieved the bottle, but then refused to hand it over and tried to break it. He was supposedly recovering in a psychiatric ward, according to the rumor mill.

The tragedy didn't end there. Of the people who then got to study it, one of them was arrested for trying to break into the lab to steal the bottle. Yet another of the scientists abruptly quit and decided she wanted to become a nun. Two more died in a car crash.

Given a number of people who died retrieving it, it wasn't long before rumors of it being cursed circulated.

A tragedy for those involved, yes, but still only a weird coincidence. Daphne didn't believe for one minute there was a curse. Scientists did not believe in magic but facts.

The fact was, because people were freaked out, she got to see the controversial bottle for herself. She took her time peeling it open, the many protective layers only adding to her excitement.

When the treasure was revealed, she took a moment to admire it, wondering at the intact stoppered jar. Not made of just any glass but a very sturdy volcanic glass shaped into a perfect urn, no handles, about twelve inches high with a narrow neck and a fat base.

The glass was a smoky gray color and smooth all over. Not a single chip or crack in it. The plug in the top of it might have at one time been a wooden cork of some kind, but it had hardened into a solid, impenetrable mass. According to the summary reports she'd read, x-rays and other tests had shown it to be empty and old. Even older than the ruins it was found in.

Hefting it in her hands, she perceived a surprising warmth and had to wonder if it was truly empty. As she turned it around, she could have sworn she heard the whisper of something shifting within.

Open me.

As if she would dare ruin such an important find. Still, she eyed the closed neck and poked at the plug. It didn't budge one bit. A wine corker would probably do the trick. Or the penknife she kept in her desk for cutting packing tape and plastic ties.

She shook her head. What was she thinking? As if she'd damage something so precious. It went on the trolley with the other artifacts, and she carefully wheeled them out to the section in the museum assigned to them.

She paid little mind to the display cases. She'd been working at the museum for more than seven years and was well acquainted with every inch.

Loved it. But sometimes she did tire of the repetitive nature of her work. There was a time she imagined her job taking her to strange places where discovery could still happen. And yes, in some of those fantasies, she had a bullwhip and a cool hat.

Alas, reality kept her in Canada, working almost fifty hours a week, showcasing other people's discoveries. Still, she didn't hate her work. She just wished it were a little more exciting.

She slowed the cart and locked its wheels, making sure it wouldn't move by accident, as, one by one, she placed the treasures in the display cases specially set aside for them. The tablet had a stand to hold it upright much like that used for decorative plates. The vase, given it was precariously balanced, had a glass box to go over it to keep it from tipping. The dagger sat on a white swatch of fabric that best showcased the detail.

Then the piece de resistance: the gray amphora. She gave it one more look. The surface reminded her of smoke, as if it moved and changed. A clever technique. She had to wonder at the skill involved in crafting something like this. It seemed impossible with the tools of the time. A true work of art.

Smash it.

The very idea rounded her mouth. Shocking. And not like her at all. What on earth was wrong with her tonight? As if she'd break such an important piece of history.

Grrrrr.

She could have sworn she heard a growl, and her mouth went dry. Just her imagination. A thing she had too much of. "There is nothing here but me and the past." She grabbed the vase. With two hands holding it carefully, she placed it on a pedestal. From above, a light would spotlight it because she'd chosen it to be the highlight of the small collection.

As she stepped back to see if she'd angled it correctly, she heard a noise almost like the flapping of fabric. Probably Frank, the security guard. She hadn't seen him on his rounds yet.

She turned a glance at the arch leading into this branch of the museum. "Frank, is that you?"

The older man often found her on his rounds to say hello and offer her the newest low-fat, no-sugar treat his wife had made him. He said that by sharing he didn't have to throw them out and lie to his wife about eating them.

Because she felt sorry for his woebegone expression, she claimed to love the no-sugar, coconut oil mixed with plain cocoa powder monstrosity. She'd then beg to take the whole thing, mostly so she could toss it out for Frank and save him.

The archway remained empty, as did the room with other tables and stands showcasing more of Canada's history. She probably imagined the noise. It wasn't as if it were hard to spook herself when working in the museum at night. Being surrounded by all that history, it was easy to let herself imagine things that weren't actually there.

Ghosts aren't real.

She should know. If ever a place would be haunted, it would the place where old things came to rest.

Turning back to the bottle, she angled it slightly then added its place card. She'd already uploaded the information for the digital display built into the pedestal. As she went to grab the glass case that she'd place over it, she heard the sound again. A rustling—from above.

Had a bird gotten into the museum again? The last one had caused trouble when it pooped on some borrowed artifacts. She'd not enjoyed explaining to the French curator why one of their marble busts had a very clean area where they'd scrubbed it.

If they had another avian problem, she'd better make sure the bottle wasn't touched. She set the case over the amphora and clipped it into place before glancing up. Smoke seeped from a vent in the ceiling.

Fire! Oh no. She whirled to look for the nearest alarm, which turned out to be by an exit. Before she could move for it, the smoke blocked her way.

Like literally blocked, moving with sinuous purpose, not behaving at all as it should. The dark cloud rippled and then condensed until it formed a shape.

And by shape she meant a handsome fellow, dressed in a suit, dark hair slicked back, expression haughty.

For a second she eyed the artifacts she'd just laid out and wondered if they had somehow drugged her with an ancient hallucinogenic, because people did not form out of smoke. Yet how could she be high? She'd not directly touched anything, and she'd been wearing her mask the entire time.

Which could only mean she must be dreaming.

The smoky-suit man spoke, his diction perfect and yet stilted. "Step. A. Side. *Human.*" The word held a definite sneer.

"Excuse me? Why should I move? You don't belong here." Even in her dream, she wasn't about to have a man order her around. She'd worked damned hard to get her position. She shoved her glasses higher and thrust out her chest—wishing she had on something more impressive than her bright pink T-shirt.

"You would dare defy?" For a moment, his shape wavered from man to shadow.

"Who are you?" Although "what are you" was probably the better question.

"We are the Shaitan."

"We?" She glanced around. "There's more of you?"

"We are legion."

"You are spooky. I don't know how you got in here, but you need to leave. Now. The museum will be open in the morning." Dream or not, she stuck to the rules. Rules and science never let her down.

"We do not obey the likes of you. Give us the amphora." He held out a hand—with six fingers. Not the only odd thing about him. His feet didn't end in shoes, but hooves. Someone was just missing his horns.

And she was obviously hallucinating hard. This entire scenario reminded her of a video game she once played. In the game, the object was to keep the treasure safe from the demons who wanted to use it to open some gate to Hell.

"You want the vase? Why?" she asked as she pulled off the mask.

"We do not answer to humans."

"And I don't give artifacts to creepy guys in my dreams."

"This is not a dream."

"Then you are definitely not getting shit from me." She crossed her arms. "Leave. Now. Before I call security."

"You would dare to threaten us?" He appeared surprised. Then angry. "You will not stand in our way."

"Actually, I can and will." To make a point she marched to the glass case and stationed herself in front of it. "This is museum property. Any attempt to take it will be considered theft."

"It is ours," Smoky Suit hissed.

"No, it's not, and even if you had a claim, go through the proper channels. You are not getting that bottle on my watch. My ass will be grass if it goes missing."

The smoky man cocked his head more than was natural. "We tire of this conversation. You cannot stop us." He moved closer, not quite walking, more like gliding, as if his feet were on rollers.

Freaky. His cologne was acrid, yet fragrant, much like a burning spice. She held up her hand. "That's close enough."

"One thing hasn't changed in three thousand years. Humans are just as stupidly stubborn. And weak." He snapped his fingers, and invisible bands suddenly wrapped around her, cinching her arms to her body.

She gasped. "What have you done? Let me go."

"We think not." The smoky man's gaze perused her, the orbs a pure black that didn't reflect anything. Pure evil. She didn't need to call upon her decades of reading horror to recognize it. "You're not an ugly specimen for your kind," he declared. It was the most frightening thing he had said thus far, followed by a look that didn't just undress her; it left a dirty impression.

Suddenly terrified—if this was a dream, it was

turning into a nightmare—she gasped, "You know what, just take the bottle and go." She'd rather deal with the consequences of its theft than the weirdness happening, or the inherent threat chilling the blood in her veins.

"You do not command us. We will take and leave as we please."

"You'd better act fast then. Frank will be doing his rounds any second. Keep screwing around and you'll have to answer to him."

"One human against us." He grinned. "Maybe we should tie our hands behind our back to make it sporting."

"Would it make a difference?"

"No." The invisible bands around her disappeared, freeing her. He stepped even closer, the sharp smell burning her nostrils, a chill creeping up her spine.

"What are you?"

"We told you, we are the Shaitan. Surely you've heard of us."

"Nope."

He frowned. "Impossible. There are stories told about us."

She shook her head.

"What of our lesser brethren, the jinn and Ifrit?"

"Jinn as in genie?" She giggled. "Those don't exist. Not outside of the movies and books. The only genie I know is blue and sings. He's friends with Aladdin," she babbled.

"Do not mention that traitor and its human!" he boomed. He swelled large enough he had a cartoon bulging body and smoke seeping from his edges.

She blinked. "That's it, no more ice cream before bed. Because there is no way any of this is happening."

"You would dare deny the Shaitan exist! Soon the world will tremble at our name and might. We have returned from exile, and this time we shan't be stopped." Smoky man stood right in front of her, a burning furnace, and yet she was chilled to the bone.

She was also done. "I want to wake up." She shut her eyes and chanted. "This is just a bad dream. I'm sleeping in my bed."

"As you wish. Sleep forever." A hand grabbed her throat with too many fingers and lifted.

She gasped and stared at a face that didn't care. Grabbed at the hand that held her, hot but not burning. She pried at it as she kicked at him.

He smiled. "Humans might cover the world like roaches, but you are weak. Easily squished. Easily conquered."

Spots danced in front of her eyes. She was dying, and since this was a nightmare, that meant she'd wake up. About time because this wasn't fun anymore. Blackness crept in as her struggles weakened and her arms fell limp.

"Unhand the female," a deep voice demanded.

She hit the ground hard and huffed in a breath. It took her a few sucks of air before she could turn her head to see who'd come to her rescue.

What she saw made little sense. Smoky Suit's feet shifted from perfectly creased slacks ending in hooves to smoke, dancing with a second set of legs encased in dark leather. The kind of pants that molded thighs and were worn by that hot Witcher fellow.

Except the dude wearing them wasn't Henry Cavill.

Who is that? Her rescuer had short, spiked, platinum hair, square, chiseled features, and glowing eyes.

Had she smacked her head when she hit the floor?

What was happening? She must still be asleep.

She pushed herself to her knees and then to her feet, keeping track of the fighters. Mr. Smoky versus Hot Pants, who'd finished his look with a billowy shirt and an honest-to-goodness cloak. It fell in a long swath from his shoulders and swirled as he kicked.

To little effect. Hot Pants might have all the moves, but they failed to connect with Mr. Smoky, who was solid one moment, a mist the next, usually when about to get pounded.

It didn't help that Mr. Smoky taunted, "Missed us! Missed us again. Too slow."

The other dude kept the same placid expression throughout, seriously intent. He hit the mist over and over, grasping nothing. He eventually muttered a vehement, "Fuck." He drew a metal rod from a clever holster built into the leg of his pants. As it pulled free, he flicked it, the stick extending into a stave that he spun just in time, as Mr. Smoky shot a fireball at the man.

The stave blocked the inferno and shattered it, scattering sparking pieces that had her covering her face. The next ball Mr. Smoky tossed was comprised of lightning, a living, seething ball of energy that hit the stave, but rather than disperse it, Hot Pants dropped the vibrating rod with another grumbled f-word.

Mr. Smoky laughed. "You are no match for us."

Rather than reply, the dude smiled. "Don't tell me they have forgotten my name." His mouth opened, and while nothing came out of it, she'd also swear something did.

A silent word that thundered.

"No!" Mr. Smoky suddenly turned solid and yelled. Probably because Hot Pants shoved his hand inside Mr. Smoky's chest.

Like literally inside another man.

Holy crap.

"Do you know me now, Shaitan?" asked Hot Pants.

"Azrael," spat Mr. Smoky. "You should be dead."

"But I'm not. Where are the others?"

"We are everywhere and nowhere. You cannot stop us," Smoky taunted.

"You said that last time. Guess you didn't learn your lesson."

"Thou shalt regret thy actions," Smoky hissed before he exploded into a yellow mist that screamed toxic.

"Don't breathe it," was Hot Pants warning before clamping his lips.

"You don't say," she muttered as she yanked the surgical mask over the lower half of her face.

The dude spoke the invisible word again, and the poison cloud turned into a half-man. The bottom half was undulating mist. Only the upper part retained any kind of shape. And it was pissed.

"Foul serpent."

"Is that the best you can do after three thousand years?" Hot Pants mocked.

She could have really used some popcorn because this was turning out to be more fascinating than a television show. She really hoped she remembered this dream so she could transcribe it into her notebook as a potential story idea. With a more capable heroine of course. One who didn't just stand around staring.

"None shall stand against the legion. And your kind shall cease to exist." More threats from Smoky.

"Not extinct yet."

"It won't be long. Soon this world will be ours," Smoky spat.

"Over my dead body," was the gravelly reply.

"If you insist. But not today." Smoky winked. "Which reminds me. This is what I came for." He reached through the glass atop the pedestal to grab the bottle, which caused the hot dude to mutter another heartfelt "Fuck."

What was so special about an old glass bottle?

Smoky shattered the glass box, retrieving the amphora, and floated upwards with it. Hot Pants dove for the display and grabbed the bronze knife. Pulling back his arm, he launched it.

The Shaitan had a split second to make a choice. Rather than shield the object, he turned into smoke, and it dropped.

Hot Pants dove for it, but she was closer. Forget all the times she'd never caught the ball. Unless catching it with her face counted. She reached for the bottle, felt the glass hit the tip of her fingers, tilt, and hit the floor with an explosive smash.

There was an exhale, almost a scream, and a rush of air so hot it stole the breath in her lungs. It actually steamed her glasses.

The shriek faded, as did the heat, leaving only silence.

Until the smugly spoken, "Two seals broken. Only five more to go." With that cryptic message, the mist that was Mr. Smoky jetted for the ceiling and sucked itself back through the vent.

Leaving Daphne with glass shards caught in her hair, ringing ears, and an odd exhilaration. Yes, the bottle was broken, and if this were real, she'd probably get fired. But this was the most epic fantasy dream ever!

And she'd enjoyed some good ones before. Flying on a dragon's back being the coolest. But confronting an ancient evil and then seeing the good guy come to the rescue? Only one thing left to finish this most excellent subconscious adventure.

She threw herself at Hot Pants, wrapped him in a hug that tugged down his head, and planted a smooch on his lips.

A kiss unreturned as he muttered, "Fuck."

Chapter Two

The first vow: No distractions

The woman plastered herself to him. Azrael did his best to not respond, but it had been so long since he'd touched someone. And she felt good.

Soft. Nice smelling. Very attractive. But he'd not planned this long to be distracted.

He set her away from him, noticing her wide eyes and parted lips. Delectable. Perhaps he shouldn't be so hasty.

No. No distractions. He was on a mission.

"Hi, handsome. I'm Daphne. And you are?" She fluttered her lashes.

"Is something caught in your eyes? Are they burning from the smoke?" The poison usually took being ingested to activate; however, it could be the Shaitan had adapted it.

Her lips twisted as she muttered, "Even in my dreams, I can't get any."

"Get what? You make no sense, and I do not have time to decipher. Do you or do you not know the location of the seals?" he asked, his English perfect. He'd had to learn it quickly upon his arrival. Had to learn about an entirely new culture a little too quickly. The difference between this world and the one he'd left behind…staggering. He had so much to learn still; he just didn't have much time.

She blinked at him. "The what?"

"The seals. The amphora you failed to protect," he explained with a hint of exasperation.

"Dude, you are not making any sense." Daphne shook her head.

That meant yet another person who had no idea of what he spoke. He pursed his lips. For a world with knowledge literally in the palms of their hands, the occupants were ignorant. They didn't know the basics. Had forgotten what some had sacrificed to keep them safe. "I am seeking the seals that keep closed the prison."

"What prison?"

"The dimension holding the Iblis."

"The Ib-what?"

"An evil banished a long time ago."

"Banished for what?"

"Ugh," he grunted as he moved away from her and headed for the dagger that had fallen on the floor. He pocketed it as he said, "I have no time to answer your questions. Two of the seals have been broken, which means they can now search twice as fast."

"And by seals, you're referring to the bottle." She frowned. "Sorry, Hot Pants, but as far as I know, it's the only one of its kind."

"Fuck." The word that most described his life escaped his lips. Three thousand years of planning, and he was failing already. He had to do better. The fate of the world depended on him.

He stomped toward the exit of this strange place, prepared to move on, only she kept pace with him. "Hold on a second. Where are you going?"

"To locate the other seals."

"Can't your search wait like five minutes? Maybe ten if we add some foreplay?" She waggled her brows and smiled.

He stared at her. "Is there something wrong with you?"

"Obviously something is wrong with me," she exclaimed, throwing her hands in the air. "Here I am, having a dream with a super-hot guy and I still can't get laid. Could I be a bigger loser?" She held her fingers against her forehead, making a straight angle.

"This isn't a dream," he uttered with a snort before turning away.

"It has to be because guys who turn into smoke don't exist."

"Only because three thousand years ago, a brave band of companions took care of the infestation, sacrificing their lives to lock them away. I shouldn't have to explain this. Do you not keep any histories?" Just how ignorant were the people in this time and place? Surely someone recalled what happened. How a group of thirteen battled and won against evil then vowed to never let it return.

Then again, it had been three thousand years, and the world had drastically changed.

For one, humans now ruled the surface. That proved to be a surprise, as was the amount of space occupied by them. Sprawling cities joined together by roads made of some malleable stone called asphalt. Power harnessed and jetted through thin wires powering inanimate objects. Buildings soared higher than even the tower of Babel. The air smelled and tasted different. Giant metal beasts flew in the air, while others lumbered on the ground. People spoke into small devices they called phones. Could see events play out on glass screens. Something called technology appeared to be more prevalent than magic.

How had this happened? When had the mages who used to rule alongside kings lost their power?

Where had the dragons gone? The elves and other folk who used to own these lands? Had the human killed them? Or did they hide?

As he left the room, the woman followed, still talking. He could have ended her ceaseless prattling but for one thing. She knew this world, and despite all he learned, there was so much he still didn't know. He needed a guide.

"Where is your domicile? Is it near?"

"Doesn't really matter, now, does it? Not like you're interested," she grumbled, shoving at the strange lenses on her face. He'd seen things like them numerous times now and had to assume they were some kind of decorative accoutrement.

"Your domicile has a bed?" he asked.

Her expression brightened. "Queen-sized."

Not something that made any sense. The queens he'd known were vastly different when it came to width and weight. Perhaps the world had managed to thrive under a single monarch long enough that she became a unit of measurement. A fascinating thing if true.

"How do we reach your abode?"

"My car is parked out back. It's like a three-minute drive this time of night if I get all the lights."

He grimaced. "You wish us to travel via mechanical chariot?"

"Er, yes. With like a few hundred horses under

the hood, and great mileage. If you'll follow me." She indicated a different direction than the one he'd arrived in. He'd gone through the front doors, blasting them open, encased in a spell of silence to ensure surprise.

"You stated your name is Daphne."

"Yup, that's me, although I am nothing like the Mystery Gang version. No red hair." She patted her head. "But I do like purple. You?" She glanced over her shoulder with a smile, then ran into the wall and bounced off before recovering with bright red cheeks.

Holding a smile, he replied, "Azrael."

"Just like Gargamel's cat."

His brow knit. "What nonsense do you spout?"

"Not a cartoon watcher, eh?"

She continued to make little sense as she led the way through a door that opened when the bar across it was pushed. It revealed a space rendered confined with stacks of boxes, but she ignored the magical vibe emanating from a few and headed for the red lettering that glowed above a door.

"What is this place?" He'd not had much time to look, given he'd come to retrieve the seal.

"Museum."

He tried to make sense of the word. "A depository for ancient artifacts, or things that represent art, knowledge, or history."

"A perfect definition. I'm going to guess English

is your second language? Which seems surprising. You speak it rather well."

"I am recently arrived to this time and place."

"And just happened to be in my museum as Mr. Smoky attacked me."

"I was hoping to beat the Shaitan here."

"How did you even know to come?"

"The moving picture screen showed an image of it. And then, once I was close, I could hear it whispering."

That caused her to pause as she placed her hand on another bar crossing a door. "Whispering? As in aloud? Because I didn't hear anything."

For some reason she lied. "Why do you deny it?" He'd heard it shouting, demanding to be freed, the moment he entered the room.

"You think the bottle was talking?" She snorted. "Let me guess, we woke it up when we removed it from the ruins."

"You should have left it alone," he grumbled.

"Oh, stop it," she huffed. "It was a bottle. Bottles don't talk."

"Unless they're a prison," he snapped but said no more, as the door at the far end of the storage space opened and a man appeared.

He was rather sizeable, his belly hanging over the belt holding up his trousers. He spotted them and yelled, "Daphne! Are you okay? I saw the broken glass."

"Hey, Frank. I'm fine. Just a little accident. I was going to grab some fresh air before I clean up."

"Who is this guy?" The corpulent fellow pointed at him.

"None of your concern," Azrael declared with a swirl of his fingers.

"I'll decide that. You didn't sign in with me." Frank put a hand at his waist and took a step forward.

"Sir, I'm going to need you step away from Daphne and come with me."

"No need for that, Frank. I'm the one who let him in. Azrael, is, um, one of the archeologists from the ruins. He wanted to make sure the artifacts got here all right."

"I don't care. He needs to have permission from the boss and sign in with me. Let's go," Frank ordered, actually expecting Azrael to obey.

"You are trying my patience." Azrael drew from the magical residue in the room, whispered a word to give it shape, and threw it at the man, who slumped to the ground.

"What did you do to Frank?" she squeaked. She went to move past him, but he snared her arm.

"We are leaving."

"Oh no, we're not. Dream or not, Frank doesn't deserve to be hurt."

"He's sleeping."

"Wake him up. Right now."

His brows drew together. "Be quiet or I'll put you to sleep as well."

Her mouth opened. "Don't you dare! That's ass—"

He drew more magic, muttered the word of power, and she began to fall. Azrael caught her before she could hit the ground. She didn't weigh much despite her feisty nature.

Confronting a Shaitan, that took guts, or ignorance. He was betting on the latter.

Only as he brushed the hair from her face did he notice a tiny shard of glass embedded in her forehead. He brushed it loose, and a bead of blood welled. A tiny wound that would easily heal. By the time she woke up, it would already be dry.

And he'd be gone. On the lookout for the next seal to appear. With two of them broken, it wouldn't be long.

Three thousand years he'd waited for this moment. He couldn't give up now. If he did, then the sacrifice made would be in vain. The Shaitan and their master would win. And when they did, it wouldn't be gentle or kind. He knew what they were capable of.

The woman in his arms didn't move, and he thought about placing her on the floor and simply leaving. But he still needed a guide for this world. Not to mention, if the amphora were considered precious ancient artifacts, worthy of display in a repository, then perhaps, this Daphne could show him the location of other museums that might have a seal hidden away in a dusty corner or on display for anyone to break.

He rose with her in his arms then kicked the bar to swing open the door. It exited into an open space behind the building with a large expanse of asphalt painted with lines. Two metal chariots sat at rest. One was boxy with writing on it. The other, small and a bright blue. It didn't take much guessing to know which belonged to the female.

Now he only had to decipher the magic that moved the chariots. Thus far, he'd allowed others to transport him, paying only slight attention.

How hard could it be?

Tossing her over his shoulder, he strode to her chariot and tugged on the handle. It didn't open. He yanked again and, when it didn't budge, pulled harder, wrenching the metal lever clear from the body. Shoddy workmanship.

Moving to the other side, he eyed the handle. It didn't open the door either, indicating perhaps some kind of locking system. But he had no key. Palpating the female, he discovered a package of something with a minty scent, a stylus filled with ink, a phone covered in a slick material that glittered pink and gold, but no keys.

He glanced at the building. They might be inside. He didn't have the patience to look.

Would a spell work?

Outside the building, the magic proved easy to grasp, and he muttered to focus the zap he aimed at the mechanism. Something whirred and clicked. He tugged the handle, and the door opened!

He smiled. Easy. Surely driving would be as simple.

A thought revised when, after magicking the car to life and eventually lurching forward when he pressed a pedal, he hit a pole that really could have been better located. A balloon exploded from the chariot and punched him in the face, and a horn blared his shame for everyone to hear.

This wouldn't have happened if he'd left the female behind. She was proving to be bad luck, and the temptation to dump her increased. He could find someone else to help him. Yet something stayed him. Just like something forced him to act and save her from the Shaitan. Big mistake. He could have let the Shaitan kill her and, while it was distracted, stolen the bottle and stopped the coming apocalypse before it began.

But no. He just had to get involved and save the human. Now the second of seven seals was broken. Only five more to go, two enemies on the loose searching, and he was wasting time.

A zap silenced the horn. The bag in his face started to deflate but he slashed it to ribbons in case it decided to cause more trouble. He shouldered open the door and emerged to stretch before he scooped Daphne out of the back of the chariot. He quickly moved from the crash before it drew attention.

A few streets away, he found another chariot with the glowing light on top of it. A conveyance for hire.

The driver, wearing a fabric headdress, opened his window and said, "What's wrong with your friend?"

"She is sleeping."

"Sure, she is. Put the woman down and walk away."

"No. She is mine." He hugged her tighter to his chest.

"I highly doubt that. I won't let you hurt her."

A strange statement. "Why would I harm her? I require her help."

"And does she want to give you her help?" The man in the vehicle pressed a button and turned away. "Dispatch, we have a situation that will require—"

Azrael tossed some colored paper through the window. "I wish to hire your services."

The man in the fabric head covering eyed the offering then Azrael. "She your girlfriend or some-thing? Had too much to drink?"

"Yes."

It seemed as if agreeing was the correct response, as the driver grunted. "Get in. Where to?"

A location was required. He pursed his lips and eyed the female.

"What if I didn't know for sure and had to find out?" he asked, handing over more of the paper to the driver. It never ceased to amaze him how fond people of this time were of the paper they called currency. In his day, jewels, precious metals, and actual tangible goods were the way to pay.

"She got a wallet? Driver's license would have it."

"A what?"

The man with the fabric hat sighed. "You really aren't making this easy."

"She indicated she resided nearby."

"Do you have any idea how many homes are in a one-mile radius? You're going to need to be more specific."

The phone he'd taken from her vibrated, startling in and of itself. He ignored it.

The driver's phone rang next. "Hold on a second while I answer."

Even with his most excellent hearing, Azrael only heard the driver's replies of, "How did you know? Are you sure? Yes, ma'am." Then the man turned to look at him. "Lucky you, your friend called with an address."

"Friend?"

"Elsie something or other. Said she'd be seeing you soon and told me where you're going."

Who was this Elsie? And how had she known he was in this conveyance? Then again, it was the first sign he'd seen thus far that perhaps the magic he'd once known that filled this world wasn't completely gone.

The chariot deposited him outside a building. When the glass door wouldn't open, a sharp yank took care of it. Then he had to decide which door to open next. There were metal ones that had no handles for him to use to pry open, and one that, with a hard shove, led him to some stairs.

He went flight by flight, seeking a place with her scent. He found it on the fifth level. Thank fuck.

Even he was starting to feel the strain of too much exertion. The door to her abode was, of course, locked. He put a finger to it and melted the lock. Upon entering, the scent of her surrounded him. There was so much to explore, but fatigue drew him to find a bed, and he discovered what queen-sized meant.

Big enough for two.

Chapter Three

Using predictive text, type, "If I were a dragon I'd—"

Inside the Silvergrace mansion, in a room with too many opinions and not enough chocolate...

Elsie hung up the phone and handed it to Babette.

"Who were you talking to?" Babette asked.

"A cab driver. He needed an address."

"For who?"

"You'll soon see," was Elsie's cryptic reply.

Once upon a time, Babette might have snapped and shaken her, but she'd learned to let someone else be the bad guy trying to get answers. "Where's Luc?" Elsie's main squeeze.

"Avoiding this meeting." A smile teased her lips. "He's picking me up in twenty-four minutes."

"You're letting him drive? I thought you took away his keys." Babette still had flashbacks of that one terrifying time they let Luc drive. "That man is a menace on wheels."

"He's gotten better. Just wait until he starts taking motorcycle lessons. I've already got three helmets for him."

"Since when can you see the future for him?" The odd thing about the lovey-dovey couple was that Elspeth—a yellow dragon with an ability to see things that hadn't yet happened—couldn't read her husband, her demon mate.

With Luc, every day was a surprise for Elspeth. They truly were made for each other. Babette especially liked how Luc took care of Elspeth. He glowered and offered to kill anyone who offended her. Had offered to conquer the world if she wanted it.

One day Babette hoped to find the kind of love that was ready to go to war and wouldn't mind mowing the lawn. Babette had tried helping their gardener for a bit. Turned out she quickly got annoyed pushing a machine around to trim grass, so she invested in some more natural methods, only to have incidents with the goats she acquired. They didn't just make good cheese; however, the indigestion...

Maybe they should try sheep instead.

Mmm. Lamb chops.

The arguing at the meeting interfered with her

mouthwatering fantasy. Welcome to a Sept emergency meeting, presided over by King Remiel, with a bunch of people all giving their two cents. Apart from the king, Elsie, Luc, and Babette, there was Aimi Silvergrace and her mate, Brandon. Her sister Adrienne with her main squeeze, Dex. As if that weren't too many, a few of the aunts were also present arguing.

Everyone had their opinion—mostly hot air—to throw in. The king drummed his fingers in impatience.

What a wonderful clusterfuck, and it all started at the meeting last week during a similar meeting with too many hot-head dragons.

Elsie leaned close and whispered, "Watch, I'm going to make their heads explode." And winked.

It began rather tamely with Elsie announcing, "I had a dream!"

The room had instantly quieted.

Remiel lifted a hand and said, "Tell us about it."

The dragons had learned to ignore Elsie's dreams at their own peril. Now that she'd stopped taking the drugs that helped her control the visions, and had Luc to act as her anchor, she'd grown more comfortable with her ability to see the future. Knew which visions would affect them most and should be discussed.

"It was a long dream," Elsie said as she stood. "A whole bunch of things happened. Some of which I can't talk about yet." She stared off in the distance. "Yeah, we really can't

talk about that." She shook her head. "Must concentrate on the here and now. And finding them."

"Finding who?" Babette took over the questioning. As Elsie's best friend—something she had no choice in as Elsie had just declared it one day—Babette knew how to draw the right information from her, as she could ramble and wander.

"The horsemen of the apocalypse, of course," Elsie said with a roll of her eyes. "They've emerged from their prison and ride the world again."

"Did you say the fucking horsemen?" Babette yell-whispered.

Elsie nodded.

"I'm in!" Aimi Silvergrace announced.

"No, she's not," countered her hubby, Brandon.

That drew a glare from his wife. "Excuse you, but you don't get to decide."

He eyed her very round belly. "Like fuck I don't. You heard what your aunt said just this morning. You could pop that sucker any day."

"People have been birthing babies since even before they started walking. They didn't put their lives on hold. They squatted, birthed, and off they went to work and care for their families."

Brandon leaned back with a sigh and rubbed his forehead. "Someone please tell her, because she won't listen to me."

It was Aunt Yolanda who patted Aimi's hand and said, "Given how you screamed when I had to remove that splinter, I don't think so. You're not going anywhere. It's too close."

"But I want to help." Aimi pouted.

"By distracting from the mission because you've got to give birth? Don't be so selfish." Aunt Yolanda flicked her.

"Ow. You can't hurt a pregnant woman."

"And you just proved my point," Aunt Yolanda declared triumphantly.

Aimi stuck out her tongue.

The king cleared his throat, and the squabbling ceased. No one quite knew what the king would do if pushed too far, and none were willing to find out.

Babette returned to Elsie's dream. "So these horsemen? Are they cute?" The most important question.

Adrienne Silvergrace cleared her throat. "Um, Babs, you do know the horsemen are evil."

"And male," added Aimi.

"Says who?" Babette asked, twirling her hair. "Because, as far as I know, no one's actually met them. Could be they're an all-girl band, cuter than the Spice Girls, and into world peace and not the apocalypse."

Yolanda offered a wry, "I think the fact one of them is called Death probably means they're not good people."

"Are they good or evil?" Babette asked Elsie.

Only to get a shrug and a mumbled, "I don't know. I just know they're important."

It was the king's wife and mate, Sue-Ellen, only one of two humans in the room, who said, "Dragons and shapeshifters are supposed to be bad, too."

The observation caused a few in the room to squirm.

Were they showing bias? Could the horsemen just be misunderstood?

"No killing, not yet, until we know intent," the king said.

Aunt Yolanda just had to question. "You are all assuming these horsemen even exist. Sorry, Elsie, but you have to admit that dream you had is pretty farfetched. It's a well-known fact that the four horsemen are a religious construct. They don't exist as actual people but a series of events big enough to have their own distinct existence."

"I don't agree." Sue-Ellen shook her head. "The horsemen have shown up in too many places. How many instances of this construct appearing in different religions and cultures does it take before we believe there's some truth in it?"

"If they do exist, then what are they?" Aunt Yolanda asked.

"It doesn't matter what they are," Elsie interjected. "What does matter are the choices made here today. If it's any consolation, in the futures where you don't act at all, you die quickly."

That snapped plenty of mouths shut.

Babette held in a snicker, and Aunt Yolanda quickly recovered her composure to ask, "If the horsemen are here, then how are we supposed to find them?"

It was Adrienne who raised her hand and waved it like a woman on fire. "Easy. Follow the signs."

"What signs?"

"Didn't anyone read the Bible or watch the movies?" Adrienne rolled her eyes. "In a nutshell, we need to find four people riding horses: one white, a red one, black, and pale."

"What's pale?" asked Babette. "Because are we talking white pale, tan, maybe even a light gray?

Adrienne huffed. "Does it matter? Jeezus, pale as in not red, white, or black. Duh. When they come, we'll know because there'll be signs of pestilence and war and death."

"That's only three," Babette pointed out.

Adrienne scowled in annoyance. "I don't remember what the freaking fourth one is, but that's not the point. The horsemen of the apocalypse are going to be noticeable."

"Um, she might have a point about them being kind of obvious. I just got a text," Aimi interjected, waving her phone. "Check it out." Aimi raised a remote and transformed the painting of dragons playing poker into a massive screen.

All eyes turned to watch. It was CNN, and it appeared to be showing drone footage of the desert and a massive sink-hole forming as they watched. From it, four figures appeared. Four cloaked figures riding boney horses.

"It's them!" Babette exclaimed.

Adrienne snorted. "You really going to believe CNN? Home of the fake news."

Aimi flipped the channel to other news stations. North American. Europe. Russia. China. Over and over, with different languages, the same video played.

Still not convinced, Adrienne pointed out, "Those horses are all the same bony color."

"And as the voice of reason, I'm going to mention that the fact it's gone viral doesn't make it real," opined Aunt Yolanda.

"You're splitting scales. Add in Elsie's dream and this is

evidence enough that they're real," was the grumbly retort of the king. "Find them."

Simple instructions that proved difficult. The drone footage only followed one of the horsemen, the guy riding north. Plodding along in the desert, a cat sitting almost in his lap. There one second. Gone the next.

All of them disappeared without leaving a trace.

That meant they had four people—erm, things —to find, and no way to track them other than via random rumors, none that led to any real leads. Even social media proved a waste with the supposed horsemen sighting being hoaxes of people trying to go viral.

A week later, they'd still not located one of the horsemen and were back for another meeting, and Elsie was being coy about her phone call. Why would she be talking to a cab driver when she had Luc picking her up?

The king sat at the head of the table and asked for progress reports, which led to a disappointing lack of news and then bickering. Remiel didn't tolerate it for long. Their golden ruler, only recently saved from a prison, raised his hand and got instant silence. "Does anyone actually have anything to report?"

Adrienne stood. "The computer program we've been running finally got hits on our targets. I've managed to capture some footage of what might be the horsemen." She raised a remote, and a hologram appeared over the large boardroom table. From all angles, they could see a figure atop a black horse in front of the tower of London.

"Are we sure it's one of them?" Yolanda asked. She stood and moved closer to the screen. "Zoom the image."

Adrienne cropped and sized the section Aunt Yolanda indicated, drawing into sharp relief a cloaked figure with a cat perched on the pommel of the horse's saddle.

"Which one is that?" Babette asked.

"Does it matter? He likes cats. I like cats, too," Elsie said with a smile. "And not for eating."

"With that cloak, who says it's a he?" Adrienne asked.

"It's a guy." Babette would know. She had a radar for the more feminine type, such as the lady riding the pale horse who happened to be the next one caught on camera, racing down the streets of New York. The hood had fallen from her head, her hands on the reins were slender, and the hair streaming behind long, blonde, and curled at the ends.

Remiel spoke. "That's possible locations on two. Have three and four been spotted as well?"

"Maybe," was Adrienne's cautious reply. She showed them images. The third might have been glimpsed in Russia, but the footage was too grainy to be sure, as for the fourth one... It had yet to surface. "That's all I've got so far."

"You have to find the horsemen," Elsie insisted. "The fate of the world depends on it."

"Then maybe you should give us some coordinates," snapped Aunt Yolanda.

"Be nice to her," Babette warned with a sharp rebuke. "Or I'll tell Luc." He didn't like people being mean to his mate.

"Everyone will be nice or else," Remiel said on a soft drawl. "Now that Adrienne has given us some possible locations, we can move toward bringing them in."

"Are we sure that's a good idea? If the fate of the world depends on finding them, wouldn't it be better to kill them the moment we do?" Bloodthirsty Aimi wasn't one to waste time. Aunt Yolanda, her teacher, must be so proud.

"You can't kill them. I said we had to find them, because they're important. If they die, then we might as well just give up now," Elsie announced. "We need them alive."

"In that case, we'll have to split up," Babette suggested.

"Agreed. I want each team to have a good balance of defense and attack. We don't know if these horsemen will come quietly," the king said, drumming his fingers. "Contact the Sept matriarchs and have those closest to the sightings readying teams." The Septs being divided by color and then, within those colors, by strength, which usually was decided by the family bloodlines.

"You need to do more than just contact those closest, Your Majesty," Brandon added quickly. "We need to make that alert wider. We've been looking for these guys for a week, and yet they were invisible. Think what that could mean if they are intent on harm. We need to ensure all the Septs and families are on alert."

Aimi nodded. "My husband has a point. If this goes south, then strike teams should be assembled and ready to move in all the major cities at a moment's notice."

"Agreed. Make it happen." The king rose, and everyone scrambled to their feet. "I want up-to-date reports on any news of these horsemen."

"Aren't you meeting with the United Nations?" Aimi reminded. She might be pregnant, but she kept on top of things now that she was restricted close to home.

Remiel grimaced. "I'm heading there now."

"Which I still don't agree with," Aunt Yolanda muttered. "Whoever heard of the King of Dragons abasing himself in front of humans."

"It's called negotiating."

"Seems an awful lot like showing our neck."

"We didn't have much a choice, did we?" He referred to the fact they'd been outed. And while some humans still believed it was an elaborate hoax, it wouldn't be long before social media and the need for people to video everything brought more evidence to light. Best they come to an arrangement with the world now before the days of hunting resumed again.

The room dispersed quickly once the king left, until it was only Babette and Elsie.

"So, bestie, are you excited?" Elsie asked.

"About?"

"The juicy secret I kept just for you." Elspeth practically bounced in her seat.

"What did you do now?" Babette asked, not without some anticipation. She and Elsie did have a good time. Why, the last time they hung out, a refinery in Texas blew up. The time before, they sank a ship, and then there was the time Babette was sleeping with the enemy and had to redeem herself.

Elsie bit her lip as she grinned. "I know where the fourth horseman is hiding."

"And you didn't tell the king?"

"I saved it for you, best friend."

On days like today, that was most certainly true. "Where?"

"Find the nerd with the dragon tattoo."

Chapter Four

The unused pajamas under her pillow: Only cute 'til woken.

Azrael strode through the market, a tall menacing shape in a cloak. People leaned away from him, but not in fear, more like awe. Some of it respectful, others overcome and sinking to their knees, heads ducked, humming respect, clasping their hands to their forehead.

He paid them no mind. Made no sign at all that he saw them.

The leather of his boots was dusty, despite the stone road he followed. The same dirt clung to his cloak. A bruise, dark as a mottled shadow, covered his cheek.

A man fell in beside him, also wearing a long swath at his shoulders, but lighter in color, cleaner, too. "Did you handle it?"

Azrael's lips pressed tight. "I dispersed it, but not before it killed an entire village."

The other man ducked his head and huffed a breath. "We have to stop it before the pieces reassemble."

"How long can we keep shredding them apart? We need a way to separate the pieces permanently," Azrael stated.

"The kind of magic that would take..." The other man trailed off and looked around them. The only thing to see were the people going about their lives.

If the menace came to this city, so many would die. Yet if they didn't act, even more would perish.

The man in the pale cloak stared at him. "You mustn't ever give up, Azrael. Promise."

"Whatever it takes."

"Even if it takes your life?"

The statement startled Daphne awake. It took a moment to realize it was but a dream. A strange one about a place she'd never visited.

Who were those men?

Azrael. A younger version than she'd met in the museum.

The place she almost died.

Am I dead?

The pillow under her cheek said no. A gaze to the side showed the glowing red numbers of her clock. Not in the museum. Home and in bed. No misty monster or hot dude in leather pants refusing to kiss her. No medieval hero or arid ancient city. Everything was a dream.

So explain the lingering scent of cardamom. Odd since she didn't particularly like that spice and didn't own anything with it as an ingredient. She sighed, and her throat ached. Was she getting sick? That would suck.

The covers rustled and the mattress shifted as a body moved.

She wasn't alone. "Oh my God!"

She dove out of bed, reaching for the baseball bat—her weapon of choice—she kept by her night-stand. She hit the floor and brandished it with a shrieked, "Don't touch me!" To punctuate her demand, she waved her aluminum protection.

"Kind of hard to lay a finger on you given where you're standing," was the dry reply from the guy in her bed.

Not just any guy. The one from her dreams. Fully clothed. Looking singularly unimpressed.

Her shoulders slumped. "I'm still sleeping."

"More like delusional. Are you always this stubborn to see the truth?"

"Care to insult me some more? Because obviously that's all I'm good for. I think." She eyed the bed, then him, finally her fully clothed self. "I assume nothing happened."

"We slept."

"Together?"

"Your bed was adequately sized for the purpose, despite the fact you thrash in your sleep."

"Excuse me for disturbing your rest." She rolled her eyes.

"You are forgiven. Don't do it again."

"Where are my glasses?" She squinted at her nightstand.

"How would I know where you keep your cups?"

His reply made no sense, other than the part where he'd obviously lost them when he kidnapped her. A good thing she kept a spare set in her nightstand. Not as cute as her lost pair, though. They were thick and sturdy for the times she fell asleep in bed with them on.

"Why do you wear those?"

"To see. Duh."

"They amplify your vision?"

"Without them, everything is just a blur."

"Do you not have physicians to correct your sight?"

"Not everyone can afford laser surgery." A girl could dream, though.

Azrael sat up and stretched. It would have been better without the shirt.

"How did I get here? Last thing I remember, we were still in the museum. We were about to leave when Frank…" Her voice trailed off. "You did something to him. Then me!" she accused.

"I put you asleep and will do it again if you start nattering nonstop."

"Nattering? If you don't like the sound of my voice, then get out." She pointed to the door.

"I've need of you still."

"Well, you're not going to get to use me. So there," she huffed.

"You speak as if you have a choice."

"I do because this is my apartment, and you're not welcome. Leave or I will call the cops."

"Ah yes, a term for your militia. I'm afraid they will be of little use to you, as not only can they not capture me, even if they could, your mundane human prison would never hold me."

She blinked. "And that was a whole lot of crazy in one sentence."

"I am going to explain this one last time. This is not a dream. I am real, as is the fact two of the seals protecting this world have been broken."

"And you are, what, some kind of guardian?" She rubbed her forehead.

"In a sense. I'd hoped this day would never come, but the moment the first seal was broken, I was called into service. With your aid, I shall locate the other seals and keep them safe. If we can keep them from being destroyed, then the world might stand a chance."

"Me, help save the world?" She snickered. Then outright chuckled. "Definitely still dreaming." She flopped onto the bed beside him, only to squeak as his body covered hers.

"I fail to see the amusement or understand why you persist in denying reality."

The weight of him pressed on her. Hot. Heavy. All man.

Her lips parted, and his gaze caught hers, his eyes a vivid green.

"Magic isn't real," she said. "Sexy as you are, you are definitely not real."

"Do I feel like a dream to you?" he asked, the words hot against her lips.

"More like a tease," was her complaint.

"Would this help you decide?" He dipped his head and let his lips brush against hers.

Lightly.

Softly.

Then more firmly, slanting his mouth over hers, claiming it. He sucked the bottom lip, finally giving her the kiss she'd been craving.

Her breath shortened, and her body tingled with awareness. Her senses heightened by his nearness. His weight. The potential for pleasure.

She was the one to stop the kiss, mostly because the pounding at the door proved most distracting. She shoved at him, and for a moment, he didn't move but buried his face in the crook of her neck.

A hot sigh moistened her skin. "I believe your attention is required."

"You don't say." With a bit of regret at the

dream determined to cockblock her, she moved to the door.

"Who is it?" she yelled.

"Police, ma'am. Please open the door."

The cops? They must have come because of the museum.

She undid the chain on her door, and yanked it open. Two uniformed police officers stood there, one with a hand on the butt of his weapon.

Seriously?

"Hello, officers. How can I help you?"

"Are you Daphne Malkovitch?"

"I am."

"Do you know a Frank Mascarpone?"

"I do. We both work at the museum. Did Frank tell you to check on me? I know he was worried about me last night even though I tried to tell him I was fine."

"You admit to seeing Mr. Mascarpone last night?"

"Yes. Why? Is he okay?" Obviously, he'd recovered if he'd managed to call the cops.

"Mr. Mascarpone was not at his post, and yet his phone and other personal effects were found at the museum."

It took her a moment to clue into what he was saying. "Wait a second, is Frank missing?"

Rather than reply, the officer fired another question. "What time did you last see him?"

"Gosh, it was late. Probably close to eleven," she answered.

"And was that on the first level in the temporary exhibit wing?"

"No. We last spoke in the storage room."

"What was the nature of that conversation? Did you argue?"

"What? No. You can't think I did something to him." Her eyes widened. "Have you seen the size of me?" She shoved at her glasses in agitation.

"Perhaps you had an accomplice."

Was that a trick question? Did they know about her guest?

"Maybe Frank is having a nap, and you just haven't found him." She'd once found him sleeping on the throne they got on a loan, and she'd promised not to report him.

"Where did you go after seeing your coworker?"

"Home. I think."

The police officer gave her a sharp look. "What do you mean, think? Do you recall leaving the museum or not?"

"I was really tired. It's kind of a blank." She shrugged. Tried a sheepish grin.

The officer didn't melt at all. "Ma'am, were you under the influence of drugs or alcohol in the previous twenty-four hours?"

"No. Of course not."

"Were you the one driving the vehicle registered

in your name that mounted a curb and crashed into an electrical pole?"

"What? No. I don't think I was." Had Azrael crashed her car? She glanced at the bedroom door. He'd yet to appear. No matter. It was time to come clean. "Listen. This is all a huge misunderstanding."

"Is what they all say," muttered the cop. "Let's just bring her down to the station and let them figure it out."

"What? No." She shook her head. "It's not me you want. See, there were these two guys at the museum last night. Although, guy might be misnomer, given one of them was made of smoke." In her panic—because good girls didn't get visited by the police—she'd babbled and said more than she should have.

"Ma'am, I'm going to ask you again, are you under the influence of anything?"

"No. I don't do drugs. And I didn't do anything to Frank. That was the second guy. Not the smoky one. The one in the leather pants."

The cop stepped to the side of her door. "Ma'am, you need to come with us."

"Why? I didn't do anything. I swear. Azrael said he only put Frank to sleep. And then he did it to me too! It's why I don't remember anything."

"Ms. Malkovitch, please step outside of your apartment."

"No." She shook her head. "This is crazy. I didn't do anything."

"So you claim, and yet the museum display in your care was vandalized, items stolen, and you admit to being the last person to see Frank Mascarpone before his disappearance."

Panic gripped her tighter than the cop's fingers on her arm.

"Wait. I'm telling you; it was not me. What happened with Frank and the museum, it was Azrael and the smoky dude. I thought it was a dream. I must still be dreaming."

"Is that the name of the drug you took? Are you high right now?" chided the cop as he flipped her around and slapped cuffs on her wrists.

Cold metal that woke her quicker than a bucket of water. This was really happening.

She was being marched out of her apartment and taken in for questioning instead of the real culprit. "Why aren't you arresting Azrael? He's the one who can explain what happened."

"Is Azrael a person?" the second officer asked, peeking inside her apartment. "Where is he?"

"My bedroom. He spent the night here."

"Call him," cop number one demanded.

She immediately shouted, "Azrael. I know you're listening. Get out here. I am not taking the fall for you."

No reply.

What a freaking douche canoe.

"Let me go get him," she offered.

"You're not going anywhere." The cop who had her handcuffed tilted his head toward his partner. "Better check it out."

The second officer slid past her, hand on the butt of his gun. Not even two minutes later, he returned, shaking his head. "There's no one else here."

"He left?" How? She lived on the fifth floor. Her bedroom window was a steep drop.

"Let's go." The officers propelled her out of the door, down the hall, and then into the elevator before stuffing her into the back of their cruiser.

Like a criminal.

She spent the next several hours telling her side of the story. Flustered, she stupidly kept repeating the truth. Everything she remembered, even the crazy parts. She also made the mistake of claiming she thought it was a dream or hallucination until she woke up beside Azrael, the man they couldn't find any proof of, which led to her being asked to provide a urine sample in a cup.

"I'm not high." She was stone-cold sober, which made it all the more horrifying.

By late afternoon, she'd talked herself almost hoarse, had her picture and fingerprints taken, and had to pee in front of someone in the cell she shared with a criminal.

The circumstantial evidence was stacked against her. According to the detective in charge, the prosecution was looking to lay numerous charges. They'd already gotten a warrant to toss her place, looking for the missing dagger she didn't have.

"Azrael took it," she said softly for the umpteenth time.

No one believed her. They all thought Azrael was imaginary, just like the man made of smoke who came out of the vents.

Her obstinate insistence was probably the reason why she got sent to the special hospital and put in a padded room.

Chapter Five

The second vow: Whatever it takes.

The woman was taken by local authorities, and Azrael felt a twinge of guilt at fleeing rather than coming to her aid. He could have fought them. Two humans against him? It wasn't even a contest, but he recognized that acting would draw attention. His mission was best served by stealth.

She wasn't worth the trouble. Let her sort things out. He had a mission to complete. Yet he stayed to watch as the law enforcers shoved the artifact curator into the back of a chariot. Roughly, which made him bristle. Where did they take her? Would she be locked in a dungeon? Tortured? In his time, the women especially were mistreated in those places.

Not his problem. He couldn't jeopardize—

Fuck.

He'd have to rescue her. Before the chariot could leave, he focused his magic and tagged it. Given his need for stealth, he followed, using the rooftops to hide his stalking presence.

The tracking magic led him to a place with lots of chariots, all sporting the same red and blue glass on the top. The same lettering too. People wearing uniforms streamed in and out of a large building, too many for him to avoid. Given he couldn't exactly walk in and retrieve the human, he skulked atop a roof across from the building and considered his next move.

He could leave. Cast a spell and go looking for the next seal. With two of them broken, it wouldn't be long before the third started singing. The Shaitan wouldn't waste time.

He waited for nightfall. As hoped, the traffic going in and out slowed considerably. That was when he made his move. Entering the place, he was confronted by a rounded counter behind which a female in uniform sat.

She eyed him with less than kind regard. "Can I help you?"

"I am looking for someone."

"Do you have a name?" was her terse rejoinder.

"Daphne. Some of your constables brought her here this morning."

"Are you family or legal representation?"

"I am"—what was he exactly to her?—"a friend."

"Well, *friend,* you missed visiting hours."

"I will see her. Now," he demanded, but this new world didn't jump to obey.

The female constable smirked. "I don't think so. What's your name?" She pulled out a pad of paper and a slim stylus.

"Your questions are tiresome, and you are wasting my time. I shall locate her myself."

Before the female had partially risen from her seat, he tossed magic at her and put her to sleep. She slumped, and he strode to a fogged glass door with a handle that had a strange mosaic above it. Some kind of intricate locking device. It zapped easily enough, and he wrenched it open, only to surprise more of the constables sitting at desks.

A few rose. One put his hands on his holster filled with a firearm, the weapon humans of this age favored. He found them rather unsporting. Whatever happened to the dancing grace of a lovely scimitar or the twirl of a spear?

He spun a shield, even as he sent out a pulse of magic. *Sleep.*

Most of the bodies dropped.

Two law enforcers, with shining eyes, remained awake. Shapeshifters. Subjects back in his day. He curled his lip. "Do not interfere." He strode forward, only to have the petite female, with canine running through her veins, step into his path.

"I can't let you through here." She put a hand on her weapon.

"You can't stop me." He could put her kind to sleep too. It just took a little more effort. Azrael gathered the magic, and the female knew it. She drew her gun and aimed just as he blew it outward.

The male dropped right away, but the female fought it, hitting the floor on her knees, the gun she held shaking.

He crouched in front of her. "Why do you fight me?" What schism changed the natural order? Azrael's view of the outside world proved somewhat limited. The prison he'd endured never really changed.

"You won't get away with this crime. There are cameras everywhere." Then softly hushed, "You idiot. Run." Sleep finally took her, and she pitched forward.

He glanced to the ceiling and spotted the cameras recording his movement. His lips pressed tight. He might have been seen. What did it matter? He'd be gone the minute he acquired Daphne.

He strode through the large room cluttered with desks, found stairs, and went down, seeking the dungeons. He quickly realized he needed to go up. More people had to go to sleep as they faced him with weapons. His irritation grew with every room he searched.

It was only as he stood in front of the cell where traces of her scent still lingered that he finally grasped he'd invaded for nothing. Daphne had been moved to another location. He'd lost her.

Fuck.

Chapter Six

A t-shirt in her drawer at home: Don't hate me because I'm smart. You need all the brain cells you've got just to breathe.

Daphne lay on the cot, staring at the ceiling. Not the stained popcorn stucco of her apartment or the lovely cell at the police station. Nope.

I am in the loony bin.

The detective in charge thought it best she be placed under observation because she was obviously crazy.

Azrael didn't exist. He couldn't because then she'd have to figure out how he escaped through a window too high to jump out of. Since that just wasn't possible, it meant she'd imagined him.

Maybe she was in the right place. She needed help. Something must be wrong with her to imagine a fake guy she'd made out with. If he didn't exist, did that make her hot and heavy kissing masturbation?

It has to be drugs. Or a brain tumor. She should get them to scan her head, make sure—

Click. Clank. The door to her room wrenched opened, and Owen, the male orderly, entered barking, "Get up, Daphne. You've got a visitor." He appeared in the same fine mood as earlier when the cops drove her over and marched her in. "You do know the hockey game is on tonight," he'd complained then.

"Do the paperwork later," suggested one of police officers. "We already signed off, so just fill in the blanks."

Owen had sighed. "Fine." He'd showed his displeasure by the way he didn't really process her. She didn't even get a change of clothes, just a thin blanket and a snapped, "If you cause trouble, I will sedate your ass."

His bedside manner actually helped her hold back the tears. Being angry at this jerk made it easier to not fall into despair.

How had she gone from having the best day of her life to looking at jail time? And now, she couldn't even mope in her uncomfortable cot because Owen had decided to return and yell some more.

"Move it." He grabbed for her arm, and she found herself rudely yanked out of bed.

"Why? Where are we going?" She had a sudden vain hope that they finally realized their mistake and were setting her free.

"Visitor."

"Who is it? I don't suppose I could get a change of clothes, maybe a toothbrush." A time like this and she found herself glancing at her bare feet, knowing her hair was a nest. She needed a shower something fierce. Her skin practically crawled.

"Do you want to see them or not?" Apparently it wasn't a question, as she was half dragged down a hall and through some locked doors.

She tried to ask questions along the way. "Who came to see me? Is it my lawyer?" Because she'd yet to see one. They kept saying a public defender would be assigned. She was still waiting when they bundled her off for a psychiatric evaluation, claiming they needed to check her mental state.

With good reason. She sounded loony tunes. A smoky man in a suit and a guy with a cloak who could climb out of a fifth-story window and put people to sleep? Completely off her rocker and in need of meds. It didn't help that the cameras that should have been recording inside the museum glitched the moment before the smoke attack. The last thing they had on video was her handling the artifacts.

It was only her word Azrael even existed. With Frank still missing and her the last to see him... Even she could see how the circumstantial evidence stacked to make her look guilty.

"You'll find out who it is in a second." The meaty grip didn't loosen until they entered a large room set with round tables and light plastic chairs with tennis balls on the feet. Cubby-style cases lined the window, filled with game boxes and puzzles.

A woman stood at the window with hands tucked behind her back, her long gray jacket cinched at the waist, her hair perfectly coiffed.

The orderly shoved Daphne away from him and left, slamming the door shut. *Click.* It locked. Leaving her alone with the woman.

The woman turned to eye her, but before Daphne could say anything, a voice from behind exclaimed, "Shit, she looks just like a librarian."

"Excuse me?" Daphne mumbled, turning around to see a second, younger woman.

"Well minus the proper pants. Blouse. Cardigan. Missing some proper shoes and glasses, too, but other than that, you totally look like you should be working for a library."

"Museum, actually," Daphne said.

"Same thing. They both have stuff that tells stories." The young woman rocked a pixie shag and ripped-up jeans paired with a cropped top. "I'm Babette. And this is—"

"None of her business. Before you start babbling, perhaps we should ascertain we have the correct person." The elegantly coiffed woman eyed her. "State your name."

"You're not my lawyer." Daphne said.

"No. But I can get you out of here, if you are who I'm looking for. So let's try this again. Who are you?"

It was Babette who snorted. "Seriously, Yolanda? You can tell who she is because she's the spitting image of her employee ID and the whole reason we're here."

The woman called Yolanda made a disparaging noise. "What if she has a twin?"

"Her file states she's an only child."

Daphne was confused. "Who are you? And why are you here?" And why did they have a file on her?

"Who we are isn't important," said by a terse Yolanda. "Were you the person working at the museum last night? The one in charge of unpacking the Lost Lake Collection." The stupid name the media gave the artifacts.

She nodded. "But I didn't do anything."

"Never said you did." Yolanda took a step toward Daphne. "You were there when the dagger went missing?"

"Yes. But I wasn't alone."

"Who else was there?" prodded the elegant woman.

Daphne almost blurted it out. How a smoky man and a guy in hot leather pants showed up in the museum. Could hear the crazy in it.

She'd never get out of here if she kept to that story. "No one was with me."

"The police report says you claimed there were two other people," Babette declared, holding out her phone and an image with lots of tiny writing.

"It's possible I imagined them."

"Let's say you didn't hallucinate. Let's say they actually existed. What did they look like? Can you tell us what they said?"

The older woman sounded reasonable. Was this some kind of trick? Maybe she was a doctor, doing a snap assessment on her mental state.

Daphne chewed her lip, debating how to reply. Lie or tell the truth?

Babette answered before she could decide. "Would it help if we said we believe you?"

"No one else does." It might have emerged a tad sulky.

"Not entirely their fault. Your story is flimsy, especially without proof those men existed. It would have helped your case if we'd not borrowed the video footage that proved your story," Yolanda blithely admitted.

"What? You mean to say Azrael and Smoky Man really existed? Then why am I in the nuthouse?" she exclaimed hotly.

Babette shrugged. "Sorry. Not sorry. We needed it more than the cops did."

"They think I'm crazy. They've got me in a tiny cell of a room without even a shower."

"Look on the bright side, you're not actually insane." Babette beamed.

That only made Daphne scowl. "Who are you, and why did you steal the video footage?"

"Still none of your business. We want to know what happened after you left the museum with the man in the cape," Yolanda demanded.

"I don't remember leaving. I think he drugged me."

"When did you wake up?" The older woman kept up her interrogation.

"This morning." It seemed like days ago.

"You were in your apartment according to the report." Yolanda appeared well acquainted with the facts of her case.

She nodded. "And I swear Azrael was with me."

"The horseman?" Babette asked eagerly.

"What horse?"

"She means the man in the cloak," Yolanda stated.

"Yes. But when I answered the door, he somehow managed to hide, and hide good, because when the cops went in the bedroom, they couldn't find him."

The two women eyed each other, as if

exchanging some communication. But Babette aimed her next words at Daphne. "Did he ever say anything about who he was or where he came from?"

"Why are you asking so many questions about Azrael?" She remembered his name with as much ease as his handsome face.

"He is a person of interest."

"Azrael is a criminal?" she exclaimed. "You have to tell the police. Once they know he's real, they'll know I'm telling the truth. That I did nothing wrong."

Babette slung her arm around Daphne and offered a squeeze. "Don't you worry that pretty little head of yours. I promise, once we find the dude in the cloak, we'll make sure your situation is handled."

"What if you don't catch him?"

"I've got you covered, babe," Babette promised.

The older lady made a sound. "If you're done flirting, can we get back to our real reason for being here?"

"Don't get your granny panties in a twist, Auntie. It's called putting the target at ease."

Daphne's eyes widened. "Target?" she squeaked. "I thought you believed me when I said I didn't do anything."

"I do. Calm down, babe." Babette tried to soothe, but Daphne pulled away.

"What if I don't want to help?"

"You don't have a choice if you want to be released," growled the lady. "So why not speed up that process by answering our questions? Starting with the men you saw. You spoke with man in the cloak. Called him by name?"

"He said his name is Azrael—"

"Like the cat?" Babette interrupted.

"What cat?" the older woman asked.

Babette rolled her eyes and said, "Gargamel's of course." Anyone who'd watched the Smurfs would understand.

Daphne shook her head. "He is not named after a feline, apparently."

"Did he give you a last name?"

"No." Daphne shifted and took a few steps toward the window. The other women didn't move or say anything. "We never got that far. Mostly, I saw him fight, thought I was hallucinating his existence, and then he put me to sleep."

"Just sleep? You implied he was in your apartment when you woke."

"He was." And she couldn't help but recall him in her bed.

"Look at those cheeks. Did something happen? If I get a doll, will you show me where he touched you?" Babette asked. "If we can't find a doll, then you can put your hands on me."

"Babette!"

It was in that moment, as Babette winked at her, that Daphne realized the shocking statement was meant to do one thing only. Drive her aunt a little bonkers. It worked like a charm.

"I can see why you're having a hard time finding someone to partner with. Really, Babette. You need to control that mouth of yours."

"But, Auntie, I do my best work with my lips. Just ask my last girlfriend." Babette purposely antagonized her aunt.

The aunt had a cool smile as she said, "Your last girlfriend? You mean the one that used you to try and harm the family with plans to take over the world?"

Babette winced. "Are you all going to harp on it the rest of my life? Yes, I slept with pure evil. Yes, I am a dumbass. Especially since the sex was only mediocre."

Daphne was a spectator to the most dysfunctional dynamic she'd ever encountered. She couldn't help but ask, "Do you always fight like this?"

"Fight?" The lady snorted. "Just a lively discussion."

"Yeah, because in a fight, things always get broken. Now, speaking of broken shit, pictures we saw of the crime scene showed a mess at the museum. Apparently, some kind of glass bottle was broken?" Babette swiped her phone and showed a marker with a number beside a jagged chunk of the amphora.

"The bottle was broken on purpose. Smoky Man grabbed it and dropped it when Azrael tossed the dagger at him."

"Smoky Man being?" Yolanda asked for clarification. As if any of this made any sense.

"The guy who came out of the vent. Only he wasn't a guy when he did it, but like some dark mist that turned into a guy." It sounded just as crazy now as when she'd told the detectives earlier, yet these two women didn't bat an eye. Rather they drew close to confer.

"Do we know of anyone who turns into smoke?"

"Nope." Babette popped the P. She eyed Daphne. "Before the knife got thrown, did they say anything about it?"

"No, they wanted the glass bottle."

"The now broken one?" The older woman sounded unsure.

She nodded.

"That makes no sense," she huffed. "What of the dagger?"

"When Smoky Man was about to take off with the bottle, Azrael threw it. But it never hit because the guy turned into a fog, and it fell to the ground."

"No knife was recovered at the scene."

"That's because before Azrael made me leave,

he put it in his pocket. Which I know I should have stopped, but in the moment, I didn't actually think it was all really happening." She still had a hard time believing it wasn't a dream.

"So this Azrael has it?"

"Yes."

"And the last time you saw him was in your bedroom?" Babette prodded.

"He was there when I went to answer the door for the cops, but gone when they checked. And I don't know how. I live too high for him to jump, and there's nothing to climb."

"Can he turn into smoke too?" Babette asked.

She shrugged. "I don't know. I didn't ask him if he could."

"He probably just hid," the older woman said pointedly.

"Doesn't matter how he hid from the cops. That wasn't cool leaving her to deal with them alone," Babette exclaimed. "What an asshole. It's why I won't date men. Chicks before pricks," she said with a fist pump. "Right, Daphne?"

"Would you please contain yourself, Babette? We are here to gather information, not for you to find your next conquest."

"She's straight, Auntie." Babette rolled her eyes. "And even if she weren't, I know how to act serious."

"Since when?" was the muttered reply. The

aunt focused on Daphne. "Any idea where this Azrael character might have gone? Maybe he mentioned an address or a place he hangs out?"

She shook her head, and only then realized she'd been hugging her body the entire time. "I never saw him before last night. And haven't seen him since this morning at my place."

"Lovely. Another dead end," Babette declared.

"Not exactly nothing," the older woman noted. "We now have a clue as to what he was after. That bottle must have been important."

"And he has the dagger." Babette nodded grimly. "We need to warn the others."

"Others?" Daphne repeated faintly. "Can someone explain what's happening?"

"Afraid not," Babette said, not looking one bit apologetic. "Family business and all that. But we do thank you for your aid."

"I helped you. Now you have to help me. Tell the detectives about Azrael."

"Eventually. We need to catch that cloaked stranger first."

"What do you mean, eventually?" Daphne exclaimed. "I don't belong here. I'm innocent."

"Like I said, sorry, but not really sorry. We can't have you jeopardizing our retrieval of Azrael. The fate of the world is depending on it and all that jazz." Babette patted her cheek as she sauntered past. "Coming, Auntie?" Babette gave a few sharp taps at the door then leaned against the jamb.

"This is so unfair." Daphne let go of her ribs to rake fingers through messy hair. The sleeve of her orange jumpsuit—courtesy of her jail stint—flopped to her elbow, the button that held the cuff closed missing.

Babette straightened and cleared her throat. "Um, what's that on your wrist?"

Daphne didn't have to look. She held out her hand and showed off the tiny tattoo with intricate detail. "It's a dragon. I got it when I graduated university."

"Change of plans," Babette barked as the door opened and her aunt made to leave the room. "The girl comes with us."

"What are you talking about? We can't take her with us."

"No shit, you can't," Owen remarked, rudely having returned to let them out. "This little jailbird can't leave because someone will notice and blame me since I'm on watch."

"Except, you didn't process her yet. There's nothing that says she ever made it here."

"Joe and Tyrone—"

"Will keep their mouths shut. Or haven't you figured out yet who told us to talk to you?"

"Taking her wasn't part of our deal."

"I'm changing the terms." Babette dug into the

pocket of her sweater and pulled out a thick wad of cash.

Owen's eyes widened.

"You never saw her," Babette stated as she handed it over.

"What if Joe and Tyrone cause trouble?"

"Maybe you should talk to them ahead of time. Give them a little something too." Babette peeled even more cash out.

Owen wandered off, whistling.

But Auntie wasn't happy. "I don't know why you went through that trouble. We are not taking the girl. She knows nothing."

Babette grabbed Daphne's arm and lifted it. "Look at her wrist."

"What of it?"

"Elspeth said I should find the nerd with the dragon tattoo. And we have!"

Yolanda's lips pursed. "We did, and because of that, we now have a name. She's no more use to us. At this point she can still walk away."

"Are you sure we're supposed to let her go? You're willing to take that chance?" Babette arched a brow.

Auntie's lips pinched so tight they almost disappeared. "Fine. Bring her. But she's your responsibility."

"You heard my aunt. We are ditching this joint."

A firm, yet gentle grip tugged Daphne, and she snapped out of her surprise enough to say, "Why should I leave with you?"

"Because you've seen one of them. The horsemen of the apocalypse," Babette stated.

"Are you talking about Mr. Smoky?"

"Actually, I meant the guy in the cloak. Elsie says it's super important we find him and his pals because if we don't the world will be in grave trouble. Rivers running with blood. Plague. Famine and all that stuff. Which personally sounds like a good time to me, except for the people dying part. I like people."

"Do you ever shut up?" snapped Yolanda.

"No," Babette sassed. "What are you going to do about it?"

"I'm going to—" Whatever threat Auntie meant to bestow got interrupted by the sudden blaring of "The Imperial March." She held up her phone and frowned. "I need to take this. But we're done here. I'll meet you downstairs at the car." Yolanda strutted away, and Babette grumbled.

"As if I am getting into a car again with her. She drives like a maniac. You and I are taking another route."

"To go where? Where are you taking me?"

"Somewhere that isn't here. Do you need to pack anything?"

"I have nothing."

Babette appeared startled. "Well, that's kind of sad. Everyone should have a hoard."

"What would I do with a horde of marauders?"

"Not that kind of hoard." Babette rolled her eyes. "I'll explain later. We really should go before someone I haven't bribed notices we're here."

"Won't I be in more trouble if I escape?"

"Probably. Good times, right?" Babette winked. "Now, let's get our butts onto that roof. I'll be able to get a better running start."

"Wait, you're going to kill me?" It was the only conclusion to draw and suddenly made Daphne wonder who Babette really was, because she talked crazy. And now implied they'd be jumping off a roof. What if Babette were a patient?

A truly insane one.

Daphne ran for the door, only Babette beat her to it.

"Really, Daphne, we don't have time to play tag. We have to save the world."

"I am not going anywhere with you."

"Ah jeez, did I give you the impression you had a choice? Really sorry about that. I've been working on my approach with people so they're not intimidated by me. I mean I can understand why they are, total awesomeness in one tiny package." She swept a hand at her body.

"I won't let you kill me."

"Why would I want to kill you? Elspeth told me

to find you. And I did. So I guess now we need to figure out our next move."

"Who is Elspeth?" And why was everyone concerned with what she said?

"You'll meet her soon. Maybe." Babette frowned. "Well shit, did I just make a prediction? Elsie must be rubbing off on me. Slap me with some grease and make me squeal like a thin-skinned newt on a hot volcanic ledge. I don't want to see the future." Babette continued to make little sense. "Let's go. Rooftop time," she sang, grabbing hold of Daphne by the upper arm in a grip that would require the Jaws of Life to break.

Daphne had no choice but to follow, up the flights of stairs. Locked anywhere, no problem, given how quickly Babette went through. Given the strangeness of the past few days, she was past wondering how she managed to do it.

As they emerged onto the roof, a deep shiver shook Daphne. Not just because of the cool night air that whipped past her skin. They were quite a few stories above ground. Alone. No one to save her when Babette shoved her off the building. Everyone would assume the crazy girl from the museum had committed suicide.

She'd die just like the other people who'd come in contact with the special collection. The curse would have another victim.

The grip on her arm loosened as Babette

released her and took a few paces. "Okay, Daphne, we have a few choices on how to do this. I can carry you on my back, but you'd have to hold on tight, and if I have to do a belly roll, you might fall off. If you don't mind a bit of saliva, then I can carry you in my jaws. But I know humans are kind of wiggy about that spot. I blame those stories about us eating all those heroes. As if we'd go after stringy meat inside a smelly tin can. Give me a nice plump ewe any day. Right after a shearing so the hair doesn't get caught in my teeth."

There was a real possibility Daphne's eyes would fall out of her head.

Babette kept going. "I'd use my talons, but they're kind of an embarrassing mess right now. I need a new pedicurist. Word of advice, if you like your nail lady, don't sleep with her. They are impossible to replace."

None of that made any sense, which was probably why Daphne was so happy to hear *his* voice.

"Step away from the human."

Chapter Seven

The third vow: Never give up.

Losing wasn't something Azrael accepted with grace. He'd not lived this long to fail. Yet, less than a moon cycle back, and he wasn't doing so well.

A seal broken under his very gaze, the Shaitan escaped, and a female in trouble with the constabulary, partly because of him. He felt somewhat beholden. Conflicted.

Should he help her or continue with his one and only mission?

As to the latter, he had no leads to follow. The Shaitan had disappeared and gone to ground somewhere. Azrael had no clue where to find the next seal, but he knew someone who might be able to help.

Daphne.

Which meant he had to rescue her. The problem being, how? And where? He could waste time questioning people and drawing attention to his target, or he could be subtle about his search for the woman. Meaning magic.

The spell required specific materials, personal items that belonged to Daphne. Hair being one of the best ingredients. He returned to her abode, once more levitating to her window and entering. The place appeared vastly messier than when he left, with furniture turned over, drawers emptied.

Someone had been through searching, and not just humans. The stench lingered, an acrid burn that indicated the Shaitan had been here. The leaking of scent was a sign it was weak from its display earlier. Good to know it hadn't gotten stronger while imprisoned.

Also good was the fact the Shaitan didn't get its hands on the dagger, now in the sheath at Azrael's waist. It didn't quite fit, and displaced his stave to a less comfortable spot at his back, but he needed the shielding the sheath provided to block the weapon's intricate power.

The knife's power came from the metal. Dracinore. It was harvested from meteors and disruptive to many forms of magic and even certain innate gifts. It was the one thing that could harm the Shaitan. But only if it was solid. The metal had no effect on it in its mist form.

As he moved through the destruction of Daphne's home, he took in more detail than he had the evening before, including the fact there appeared to be many dragons. Crystal ones. Porcelain. Art on the wall. Stitched into cushions. Serpentine. Plump. Some winged beasts, some spiked. What an interesting hoard.

He'd given up his hoard when he went willingly to his prison. He'd owned a lovely collection of rocks. He'd visited it out of curiosity and been saddened to see it some kind of attraction for humans. They arrived in long chariots, dozens at a time, aiming their little boxes, pointing and chattering about the magic of the place.

Little did they know it was just one of a few places he'd marked out as the perfect nap spot. He used to hoard sleep. When he wasn't battling the Shaitan, he would find one of his special rings of stone and rest.

He wished he'd known he'd have three thousand years to sleep. He would have done more.

He realized he was stroking a dragon, a fierce specimen made of green jade. The horns were intricate. The detail quite accurate.

He pocketed it and moved to the bathing chamber. He didn't need too much, a piece of clothing bearing her scent, a few strands of hair. Once he'd gathered a few things, he placed them in a pile, adding the jade dragon to sit atop it. His hands came together as he bowed his head, pulling at the magic in the air.

It felt so good to have access to it again. Three thousand years he'd spent cut off from the source, and now he could dip into it.

The spell took shape, a complicated blend of her essence and magic. He twisted it all together to create a special pulse. It hovered in the air, slowly blinking. It needed a container.

He found a strange oval-shaped object under the sink. It popped open when squeezed, the inside the perfect size for the pulse once he removed the rubbery item shaped as a mini cup with a stem. It stank of blood, as did the case, but that would only amplify the tracking spell.

As he came out of the bathing chamber with the pulsing case in hand, his gaze was caught by the bed. He'd been tired when he'd collapsed in it with her. Using magic had a price. Yet as fatigued as he was, he'd remained aware of her. When she moved, he noted it.

The pulse in the case intensified for a moment as his hand tightened around it. For a second, he could swear he saw her, expression frightened, her arm being gripped by a man.

Who was he? What did he want with her?

Azrael had to hurry. He eschewed regular

methods to leave via the window again. With the pulse of magic as his guide, he sped across the city, wings of shadow at his back. He didn't fear being seen, as the hour was getting late. Most humans slumbered or shut themselves away. Night and its shadows reigned, meaning none saw the dark mass overhead. But he saw everything, and the pulse in his grip thumped faster.

Close now. In the distance, he spotted the two figures on the edge of the roof. He'd found Daphne in the company of a stranger, and when she bolted, he realized if he didn't hurry, he might lose her for good.

He alighted on the rooftop, cocooned in silence, neither of the people present noticing his arrival. Daphne struggling in someone's grip made him snap, "Step away from the human."

The other female with shaggy hair and a cocky attitude perused him. "Who the heck are you?"

His nostrils flared, and he angled his chin. He knew that scent. He'd help banish them for crimes against his people. "You do not get to ask me questions, silver." In his day, those belonging to the Silver Sept were the lowest of the low.

"I don't suppose your name is Azrael?"

"I am, meaning you do know who I am, and are being intentionally insolent."

"Actually, I don't know who you are. Finding out is part of my mission. So before I get testy, because it is that time of the month, who are you, why are you here, and where are your friends?"

"I don't answer to traitors," he spat. Three thousand years and he still recalled what the Silver Sept did. It was their fault he'd sacrificed his life and freedom. Them and their hunger for power. They were the reason the Shaitan entered their world.

"Holy drama. I was just asking the basics." The female angled her head. "Seriously. What are you?"

Daphne answered for him. "The jerk who ran off and left me alone to deal with the cops."

Did she imply cowardice? "I did not flee." At her pointed glare, he amended, "Merely remained out of custody that I might retrieve you later." She didn't need to know that initially he'd not actually planned to return.

"You took your sweet time rescuing me then. I've been locked up since this morning," she complained.

"You were not easy to locate."

"No, she wasn't, and I got here first," stated the stranger. "You know what they say, finders keepers. Daphne is coming with me."

"She will not go nowhere with you. *Silver*." He couldn't help but sneer. The temerity of thinking she was above him.

"Watch that tone, Azrael. My name is Babette Silvergrace, and I am a favorite of the king."

"Since when do we have a king?"

"We?" The silver cocked her eyes and frowned. "You're a dragon? What Sept do you belong to? Which family do you come from?"

"I have no family. No allegiance to any self-professed king or country, merely a vow to protect the world," he stated. When he'd gone into service so very long ago, he'd not really understood just what that meant, what he'd give up.

Too late for regret now.

"So you're a freelancer?" she asked.

"Hardly free," he said with a grimace.

The silver dragoness, wearing her human form, eyed him. "Nice cloak. Where's your horse?"

"My steed did not make it out of the desert." And proved impractical in a world where machines took their place.

"Did it at least have a name?" Daphne muttered, rubbing her forehead. "Seriously, why are we talking about a horse? We need to leave. At least I do, so I can figure out how to prove you stole that knife, not me." She jabbed a finger in his direction.

"It's not theft given it didn't belong to your museum."

"It belongs to the government, and they loaned it to a museum they own," she argued.

"I have need of it."

"Funny thing, so do we," declared the silver. She eyed him. "What are you planning to do with it?"

"Keep it out of the hands of those who would use it for the wrong purpose. Like power-hungry silvers." He glared at her.

"Dude, chill. I don't know why you've got a hater boner on for me and my Sept, but seriously, whatever grudge you have probably happened like ages ago. Get over it."

Had the silvers' status changed? Very possible given it had been a few thousand years.

"You know what that dagger can do?" the silver asked.

"Probably more than you," was his rejoinder.

Daphne clapped her hands. "I don't know what's so special about an old dagger, so care to let me in on the secret? Is this some kind of archeological rivalry?"

His vehement no was echoed by the silver. At least she showed the common sense not to tell the humans about their weakness to a certain kind of metal.

"You will stay out of my affairs, silver."

"No can do, horsey man."

His brows rose. "You dare insult me? Your irreverence is staggering."

"You're one to talk, trespassing on our territory without permission."

Daphne, following the back and forth, had enough. "You two obviously have some kind of unfinished business between you that doesn't involve me, so I'm going to leave."

"You stay until I say so." Babette grabbed Daphne by the arm.

"I laid claim to her first." He shot out his hand and, without touching her, dragged her out of Babette's grip.

Both women turned wide eyes on him, but Babette was the one to gasp, "What did you do? Because, if I didn't know better, I'd swear you used magic."

"What else would it be?" he huffed. "Do they not teach you fledglings anything in this era?"

"Magic was banned," Babette announced. "A long time ago."

His brows rose. "Banned? By who?"

Before she could reply, an alarm sounded, strident and causing humans to yell from the ground below.

The silver leaned over the edge of the parapet. "So much for my bribe. That bloody orderly has sounded the alarm. Time to leave."

"Agreed. Daphne comes with me," he stated.

"Whatever. Doesn't matter to me since you have to follow me and report to the king."

He angled his chin. "I don't have time to indulge in your king's petty delusions of grandeur."

"You don't have a choice."

"I don't listen to traitors." He went to grab

Daphne's arm, only she ducked out of reach and shook her head.

"How about I go with neither since we're on a rooftop and the only way off of it is down."

"Or up." Babette grinned. "Come on, don't tell me you haven't figured it out yet."

"Figured what out?"

"How do you feel about dragons?" Babette winked. "Try not to scream in too much excitement as I dazzle you with—" The silver's voice trailed as Azrael shed his form and expanded. And kept expanding, his advanced age making him bigger than the silver by far. Usually his magic constrained his weight, and yet now that it was released, the building creaked and cracks appeared on the surface.

Daphne stared, mouth wide open, shocked, before exclaiming, "You're a dragon!"

He was much more than that. But that explanation could wait for later.

While the silver gaped, he drew Daphne close, twining her in strands of magic against his chest. A place where she could do him no harm. Only the most trusted ever got to ride on the backs of dragons. He never trusted anyone that implicitly.

"Holy shit," Babette huffed. "You're a dragon. And those horns mean you're a mage. Oh, fuck me, the aunties and everyone else are all going to flip."

As if he cared about what silvers thought.

The door to the rooftop slammed open. "Time to go! Follow me." Babette transformed quickly and launched herself with a loud trill.

He bunched his legs and propelled himself as well, ignoring the cracks from his departure and the yells of humans on the ground, mere specks that weren't worth his attention.

He might have ignored them better if they'd not fired upon him. He uttered a sound more of surprise than pain as tiny metal chunks blew through the thinner skin of his wings. He lifted himself higher on the drafts, out of range, flanked by the much smaller silver dragon who'd tried to steal his human. Follow her indeed.

He chose his own path, only to hear her annoying trill. The silver thought to get in his way. He banked away from her and breathed magic into the space ahead of him, slicing open a portal that took him elsewhere.

Chapter Eight

Ninety-nine bottles of beer on the wall is not enough beer to get a dragon drunk.

"Five minutes!" Auntie railed. "I left you alone for five minutes, and not only did you lose the girl with the dragon tattoo, you found the horseman we're looking for and misplaced him as well."

"He's not a horseman," Babette mumbled. No. It was much worse.

Her aunt sobered. "Are you sure he was a dragon mage?"

"Know of any other dragons that have horns?"

"Perhaps he's special?"

"He did magic! And he's the biggest fucker I've ever seen." It made her feel small. Insignificant. And curious. How did a dragon mage fit into the horsemen of the apocalypse theories?

Her aunt Yolanda paced. "I'm still trying to figure out how you didn't realize what he was."

"Because he doesn't smell like one of us." Babette paced the balcony to their safe house. She'd arrived before her aunt, who'd ranted about the humans who tried to detain her. She'd had to pretend she was a doctor in order to get past security.

By the time they realized she lied, Auntie had flown to safety and now berated her niece.

"What did he smell like then? Or does your nose not work?"

She wrinkled it. "His scent was weird. Like spicy. Kind of reminded me of cinnamon but not."

Auntie latched on to that detail. "Could it be cardamom?"

"Maybe. What does cardamom even smell like?"

"Like the king's brother. Remember how Samael's scent changed when he came into his magic and horns?"

"Samael is wearing baby cologne compared to this dude. Not to mention, I didn't even smell him until he spoke. It's like he was invisible or something. A cloaking spell, obviously."

"No, not obviously," Yolanda snapped. "How is it that a dragon mage even exists? They're supposed to be extinct."

Banished, to be exact, for some major crimes

against their kind. They'd been imprisoned in another realm, where they'd more or less died out.

"Maybe Azrael, like Luc, found his way over here from another universe. Doesn't really matter how he got here."

"You're right, it doesn't matter," Yolanda muttered. "What's important is the fact we have not one but four dragon mages returned. Who knows what kind of damage they'll do."

"You think they're all dragon mages?"

"I think it's safe to assume."

"You know, I'm kind of disappointed," Babette claimed. "I always expected wizards to wear pointed hats and toss fireballs. At the least have an epically long beard."

"No self-respecting magic user would wear a beard. Much too flammable. If the horsemen are all dragon mages, then that would explain why in all those prophecies they're the harbingers of destruction. If they're anything like their banished brethren, we are in grave trouble. We need to find the one you lost and contain him before he can cause harm."

"Good luck with that. I don't think that guy is going anywhere he doesn't want to."

Few people impressed Babette, which was probably why her aunt sobered. "You said he disappeared into thin air?"

She nodded. "More or less. It's like he entered a

spot of pure shadow, and poof, he and the girl were gone."

"If he can use magic to move about, then that will make our task more difficult. What does Elspeth say?"

"Uh." Babette paused. "I don't know. I haven't talked to her since she told me to find the nerd with the tattoo."

"Then call her. Maybe she's had some kind of vision or——"

Babette's phone rang. She eyed the display. "It's Elsie." She answered, listened, and nodded a few times. Arched a brow then hung up.

"Well?" barked her aunt. "What did she say?"

"Said to sit tight and wait."

"Wait? For what?"

"Apparently, something about a side quest, necessary for the future, blah, blah. Basically, our target is going to be buried for the next day or so, so we're supposed to relax, order some pizza, and watch the next season of *You* on Netflix."

"I hate waiting," Yolanda grumbled.

"But you love that psychopath Joe," Babette cajoled.

The balcony door slid open, and a local dragon, barely an orange, with freckles across her nose, beckoned. "Come quick. You'll wanna see this. Babette made the news."

Not just Babette. Someone on the scene had

managed, with a shaky video aimed upwards, to capture not only a small silver dragon launching from the medical facility but the massive shadowy one that might have been invisible if not for the visible human strapped to its chest.

No surprise, the trending headline overnight became, Dragons Stealing Women to Make Babies. #stoptheserpents

A phone rang. Actually all of them did. Forget waiting. the king ordered them home.

Chapter Nine

A t-shirt she'd have to buy: Dragon Rider

Dragons were real.

It wasn't a hoax. And one of them had strapped her to this chest and taken off into the sky with her.

Daphne, understandably, lost her shit. She had reason. They flew with nothing holding her but invisible bands. What if the magic stopped working? Or his attention wavered?

"Oh my God." She was going to die! She turned her head and did her best to not look or think about the ground that she'd end up landing on and exploding into hamburger meat.

Wait, was that how dragons tenderized their meat? Was his plan to eat her?

Why else kidnap her other than as a snack?

Because she certainly wasn't a princess for him to guard.

All the D&D games she'd played required the dragon to be slain. Meanwhile, she couldn't help but recall the man the dragon could be.

No wonder he'd shown no real interest in her as a woman. She probably seemed too mundane. Too human.

So why did he come to her rescue? She didn't understand and yet couldn't help being giddy. She had met a dragon. The species had been an obsession of hers, even before the media reported they were real. She'd honestly not believed them. They got it right for once.

They no sooner took off than she heard gunfire. Did they not see her? How could they shoot him?

She could have sworn she heard a voice in her head. *Close your eyes and sleep.*

Next thing she knew, she woke, still in the grasp of a dragon. Via faint moonlight, she noticed they flew over flat fields and lumpy treetops, with the occasional swoop as the dragon skimmed over a hill.

She couldn't have said how long the flight lasted, only that she'd finally begun to enjoy it when the dragon alighted atop a jutting hillock. The magic holding her released, and she found herself with her bare feet on the ground. She had no socks or shoes. No sweater over the orange monstrosity she wore. The grass proved dewy and chilly, but solid.

She'd not died.

She'd have to get the t-shirt. If she ever escaped her captor.

Rather than antagonize him, she stared at her toes and the ground. As if a dragon would be ignored. It blew a hot puff of air that smelled both fragrant and terrifying. All the stories she knew had dragons eating people with a preference for the virgin type. Despite having lost that cherry awhile ago, when the dragon stirred, panic set in, and her giddy inner nerd caved to her less adventurous side.

She crouched, hands over her head, and wailed, "Don't eat me."

"As if I'd ruin my palate and digestion. Humans are the least tasty of creatures."

A peek through her fingers showed the dragon had disappeared. In its place stood Azrael, wearing his clothes, looking as grim as ever.

"How did you do that?"

"Do what?"

"Go from giant sized to man, and wearing clean clothes. Do you carry a suitcase around with you?"

"You're babbling again."

"Can you blame me? You're a dragon," was her vehement exclamation.

"You noticed?"

The sarcasm helped with her fear, and she stood. "Kind of hard to miss."

"My understanding was humans knew about dragons."

"We do, but the news never said dragons were people. Just that they existed. How is it possible? I mean, the mathematics of it. You were huge. And now you're…" She waved a hand.

"If you say small, I might revise my stance and eat you."

Given the quiver between her legs, she almost said please do, but she highly doubted he meant the favorable kind of eating. Why, look at him with his flaring nostrils and glare. He looked quite angry.

And sexy.

She pressed her legs tight. "I'm just surprised is all. I mean I heard the stories about dragons being seen, but none of those reports ever said you can also go around like regular-looking humans."

"Hardly human." He sneered.

"Or polite," was her rejoinder.

"You are hardly one to speak of manners. In my day, there was respect for your betters."

"In your day, did women get to vote?"

"Vote for what?"

She rubbed her head. "Forget it. Where are we?"

"Somewhere."

She sighed. "And why are we somewhere?"

"I am looking for something."

"Your vagueness is really helping," she snapped.

He frowned at her. "Your disrespect is grating."

"Did you expect me to bow and scrape?" She arched a brow. "You might be a dragon, but you're also being a jerk. You've tossed my life upside down, scared the hell out of me, and refuse to answer any questions. You're lucky I'm still talking to you."

"Feel free to stop. Anytime."

She glared.

He didn't seem impressed. But he did mutter, "About time you quieted." Then he had the nerve to snap his fingers. "Follow me."

She didn't budge and crossed her arms.

It took him only a few paces before he noticed. "I said, follow me."

"I'm not a dog to jump when you command."

"Then stay here."

He turned to leave, and it occurred to her that being alone might be worse. She went to follow and winced as the rock underfoot dug into her soles.

"What is wrong now?" he exclaimed.

"Don't get snippy with me. I have no shoes, in case you hadn't noticed."

He eyed her feet then narrowed his gaze on her. "Are you asking me to carry you?"

"No. I want some shoes."

"I cannot conjure shoes. My magic doesn't work that way."

"No, it's only good for being an invisible bully and forcing people to obey you."

"The powerful rule the weak."

"Maybe where you come from. Here, the strong are supposed to care for them."

"Why?"

"Because it's the nice thing to do."

He stared at her. Didn't reply, but he did glance at her feet then the path down the hill. "Give me your feet."

She blinked. "I think I'll keep them."

"Do you want protection for them or not?"

"You already said you can't make me shoes."

"I can't. But I can shield your flesh to make walking painless."

The offer intrigued, so she lifted a foot in his direction.

"Lift it higher."

She arched a brow. "That's not happening. I'm not that athletically inclined. You want my foot"—she wiggled it—"then get on your knees to work with it." It was bold of her, and yet he slowly crouched.

His hard glance was softened by a wry smile. "Congratulations. This is the first time I've knelt for someone. Don't get used to it." He gripped her foot.

Only when it began to warm, did she think to ask, "Will this hurt?"

"Horribly," was his reply.

She would have yanked her foot from his grasp, but he kept his grip firm, and as the heat intensified, it tickled. Enough that she laughed. "Stop it."

"See how this feels." He released her foot, and she set it down quickly.

Then rocked on it. "I can't feel the ground," she remarked.

"You're welcome." He held out his hand for the other one, and she let him grab it, hoping he didn't notice the shiver. Another warm tickle and it was done.

"Thank you," she said.

"Can we go now?"

"Lead the way, oh mighty dragon."

He uttered a derisive snort as he set off at a hard pace. She did her best to follow, but she wasn't a mountain goat. While her air cushion shoes didn't really slip, she couldn't say the same for her balance. She wobbled quite a bit and eventually took to sitting on her ass to go down the steep incline. Azrael strode as if gravity didn't concern him.

When a dislodged rock bounced past, he finally turned and frowned. "What is the problem?"

"I'm not keen on falling, and apparently you're not into offering a helping hand," she grumbled.

"Never occurred to me you'd need help walking." His sarcasm didn't improve her mood.

"I've had enough with your insults." She dug her feet in.

"It wasn't an insult but a statement of fact. Why must you be so contrary?"

"Why can't you be nice?"

"I haven't killed you. That *is* nice for me."

"Are those the only choices in your world, kill or not?"

"When you think you'll live forever, death does become an obsession," was his cryptic response.

"It would help if you'd at least explain why you're dragging me along with you."

"I don't understand this world."

"Or women," she muttered.

He glared.

She smiled because she knew it would annoy him.

"Nothing is as it should be. Which is where I thought you might be helpful, in helping me to understand the vagaries I'm facing."

"You want me to be your guide to the world?"

"In a sense."

"How do you not know anything? Have you been sleeping or something?"

"Or something," was his vague reply.

"For how long?"

"Three thousand years."

Holy crap. She blinked at the number. "No way. You're lying."

"Why would I lie?" Uttered with a terseness that turned into exasperation. "Had I known I'd be locked away for such a long period of time, I might have refused. Especially since dragons appear not to have inherited the Earth."

"Not only did your kind not inherit it, until recently, we all thought your kind was a myth."

"Which makes no sense. Surely your legends speak of us?"

"They do." She nodded. "As monsters to be killed."

His lips flattened. "There is much I need to understand, and you will teach me."

A three-thousand-year-old dragon chose her to help him. Kind of flattering. Until she remembered the fact she'd gone to jail because of him. Been accused of being nuts and locked in a padded room.

Suddenly, not caring who and what he was, she rose and stalked toward him until she could jab him in the chest. "Why should I help you? You abandoned me. Left me alone to handle the cops."

"I didn't have time to deal with your human laws."

"I needed you to show them I wasn't crazy, and instead, you hung me out to dry."

He blinked at her.

"It means you screwed me over."

Still more blankness. He didn't get it. The three-thousand-year-old dragon might speak perfect English, but he had lots to learn.

She sighed. "You make it hard to stay mad at you."

"Why waste the energy? The sooner you accept you're helping, the quicker we'll get things done."

"And what if I said no?" She didn't like the way he kept assuming she'd do what he asked.

"You won't."

"Will helping you hurt me?"

"Probably not."

"What do you mean probably not?" she squeaked.

"I can't guarantee you will be safe, not if the silvers are involved."

"Not exactly reassuring."

"Would you prefer I lied?"

She pressed her lips into a thin line. "You want to learn, then let's start. What do you need to know?"

"Everything."

For a man who'd supposedly been hidden away for three thousand years, he knew more than expected. He wanted broad strokes of how things worked. What did humans know of dragons and other beings? He was especially interested in the fact that the exposure of shapeshifters, dragons, and other cryptid beings had only happened recently.

"Finding out dragons were real was a shock," she admitted.

"It shouldn't have been. There was a time we

were worshipped by humans. How is it you lost all knowledge of our existence?"

"Not all. I told you, dragons are in our stories."

He made a face as they walked through some woods. "As villains and mindless beasts. We were lords. And yet now, humans are the ones governing."

"If you want to know your history so badly, then you should talk to Babette."

"Who?"

"The woman on the rooftop. The one who was going to kidnap me until you arrived."

"The silver dragon." He scowled some more. "How do you know her?"

"I don't. She showed up just before you did and asked me questions about you and the dagger then tried to kidnap me. Apparently, some woman called Elspeth told them to find me and you."

"A seer sent her? That would make sense," he mused aloud. "That would be a useful person to speak to. When we lost Maalik, we lost all glimpses of the future."

"You knew someone who predicted the future?"

"Yes, and do you know how demoralizing it is when they suddenly disappear, unable to handle what they saw?"

"So it wasn't just you locked away for three thousand years?"

"No."

"How many of you are there?"

"Only four remain." His head drooped.

"How many did you used to be?" Slowly but surely, she was putting together a picture of Azrael.

"Many more. But three thousand years awake in a prison is too much for some."

"Prison?"

"Enough. Your ceaseless prattling is annoying."

Or was he peeved he'd said more than he intended?

Having reached the bottom of the hill, he stomped through the woods, and she couldn't help but fall into a pensive state, wondering who he was. Gruff and arrogant. Yet there was something about him. Something good.

She must have been staring too long because he snapped, "Would you stop it!"

Rather than blush and apologize, she lifted her chin. "If you mean staring at you, then no. I won't. You're the first dragon I've ever met. I'm curious."

"You hoard dragons."

This time she knew what he meant. "I collect them, yes."

"Why? Why if you thought we weren't real?"

"Because of all the mythical creatures, you just seemed to be the most majestic, the most powerful."

"We were. Are."

"I don't know if I'd say that. I don't get the

impression there are that many dragons left in the world."

"One dragon is worth a hundred humans."

"The Earth has billions of us."

The number caused him almost stumble. "Billions? Impossible."

"It's true. Unless there are millions of you, we outnumber you, and we have weapons."

He stared at her. Face blank. Tight. "Weapons that won't help you against the Shaitan."

"How many are there?"

"Enough to cause misery."

"Meaning they a threat to humans."

"They are a danger to everything. They devour life. Thrive on chaos."

"How do we stop them?"

"With great sacrifice," he snapped.

He started moving again, but she wasn't about to let him stop there. "How come you keep accusing me of knowing nothing, yet when I ask you questions, you give me cryptic answers?"

"Because."

"Because is not an answer."

"And yet that's all I'm going to give you." The last thing he said for a while as he led the way through an ancient forest, old enough it gave her the creeps and she kept close. He might be annoying, but he was also big and capable of defending himself.

She was following so closely that she slammed into him when he suddenly stopped. "What the heck?"

"We're here."

"Where is here?" Because the forest looked rather the same as the other spots they'd walked through.

"We are in a place we might find answers."

"It's the middle of nowhere."

"Exactly." He knelt on the ground and blew. That was the only word she could use.

He opened his mouth, and something came out, a mist, a haze. It soaked into the ground, and he exhaled a word next. Something guttural and short.

The trees shivered, branches quivering and leaves rustling. A sudden breeze, only it didn't stop, and she began to shake as well. Actually, it was the ground shaking and groaning. Dirt crumbled and rippled as a rectangular section fell away, sinking inwards, leaving a hole in the ground with stairs leading down.

Dark stairs.

Gulp.

And what did the dragon say?

"After you."

Chapter Ten

The fourth vow: Together we are stronger. (A pity they forgot that after the first few centuries).

Azrael didn't need to smell her fear. He could see it in the way her eyes widened and her already pale skin blanched. The violent toss of her head only emphasized it.

"No way am I going into that hole."

"Why not?"

"Why don't you go first?"

He rolled his shoulders. "If you insist." He stepped onto the first step.

"Maybe I'll wait up here."

"As you wish." He'd gone down several more steps when the first howl cut the air.

"What was that?" she huffed.

"A guardian, I would imagine."

"What kind of guardian?"

"If they've bred true since my time, wolves."

"Will they attack?"

He glanced over his shoulder. "Probably. We are, after all, entering the tomb of their master."

"What? Why would you do that?"

"Because I have need of information. Would it help if I mentioned we are safer in here than out there?" Not entirely true but it got her running down the steps, not past him but tucked close.

"I liked you better when I thought it was a dream," she grumbled.

Whereas he liked her more and more despite the fact she never shut up. She wasn't like the humans he used to know. Timid bunch too much in awe of him to show any kind of true personality. In his time, none had ever dared argue with him.

He glanced down at Daphne, her shorter stature bringing out a protective instinct. She'd asked him before if she was in any danger, and he'd told her not really. What he failed to mention was he personally wouldn't let anyone harm her. Not without doing something to prevent it first.

He preferred to not speculate on what that said about him. His mission should be more important than anything. Certainly more important than a woman.

When a second howl erupted from the top of the stairs—the sound echoing down—she tucked closer, and he slid an arm around her shivering frame. "Fear not. They won't dare harm you while you are in my care."

"And if you die?"

"Then I'm told it's usually quick."

"We need to work on your reassurance speech," she muttered.

They descended the stairs, step after step, going straight down. The howling was left behind. The clomp of their feet and puff of their breath the only noise in this confined space.

She'd been quiet for the longest time before she finally asked, "Where's the light coming from?"

Not a question he'd expected but easy enough to answer. "A spell set within the very stone itself and activated by our presence." He ran his finger along the wall, and the space around them grew brighter.

"Who's at the bottom of these stairs?"

"A dead man."

"And why do you need to see him? Are you a grave robber?"

He snorted. "I have no need of things." But knowledge, that was different.

The stairs went deep, not as deep as his last prison but enough even he felt uncomfortable. Not that he showed it.

She edged closer to him, and her steps stumbled. She didn't have the same stamina as him. He swept her into his arms.

"Put me down.

"You are tired."

"That doesn't mean you can just cart me around."

"Then stop me."

"As if you'd do anything I asked," she grumbled.

"A dragon doesn't obey the dictates of a human."

"Your disdain for me and my kind is clear. I imagine I can only seem young and ignorant to one as old and senile as you."

It took him a moment to see the insult, and he laughed. "Do I seem decrepit? I assure you I am virile still."

"Says you."

"Are you still disgruntled because I chose to not fornicate with you? I have no time to be distracted thusly."

Her mouth rounded. "I am most certainly not trying to have sex with you."

"That wasn't what you said the evening we met."

"That was when I thought you were part of my dream. In the real world, I don't screw around with jerks."

"Name calling because I am a male of strong conviction?"

"Would it kill you to be nice?" she asked, glancing at his face.

Their eyes met. He slowed and set her down. "Nice isn't necessary."

"It is if you want my help."

He stepped into her, forcing her against the wall.

Her chin tilted. "You don't scare me."

"Liar." He could hear the rapid pulse of her heart. Scared. Of him. But he could also smell her arousal.

He moved closer. Or she did. Didn't matter. Somehow their lips were close. It would take only the slightest bend to kiss her.

A hot breeze flitted past, acrid and disturbing.

He stepped away from his human distraction and muttered a very low, "Fuck."

She licked her lips and looked away from him, down the remaining steps. Her voice was breathy as she said, "How much farther?"

He skipped down the stairs, lighting the tunnel at the bottom before announcing, "We're here." And their arrival hadn't gone unnoticed.

He straightened his cloak, ran fingers through his hair, and stiffened his spine before marching deeper, the sigils of magic in the wall flaring bright at his arrival, not actually meant as light sources but as a deterrent.

Keep out. Stay away. Go back. A part of him wanted to because the farther he went, the less he could touch his magic. The more he worried about what he'd find at the end of the tunnel. Three thousand years was a long time. Perhaps all was forgiven.

The knife narrowly missed his head.

"Basil." He held out his hands. "It's me, Azrael."

"As if I wouldn't know your face. I've had an eternity to think up ways to ruin it."

"Don't be angry."

"You said you'd return," a voice growled from the shadows that clung to every corner of the crypt. There was no door. Why bother when its occupant couldn't pass the spells binding him inside these walls.

"I meant to, but events conspired against me." He stepped farther into the chamber. A prison even worse than his own.

"And it took you three thousand years to find the time?" The voice echoed from his left, yet he could see nothing amidst the piles of junk. Mounds of it. Jewelry and rotted cloth. Even bones stripped of their meat.

"You kept count?"

"What else would I do?" rasped the man.

"It's not as if I had a choice. I was a prisoner as much as you."

Only now did he see movement as Basil finally stepped from his hiding spot. He wore a hooded cloak, tattered and patched with skin and fur from whatever creatures he'd managed to trap.

"It was claimed that you and twelve other idiots thought you had the answer, yet my pack tells me the Shaitan roam again."

"It is because we knew we couldn't trap them forever that we sacrificed our freedom."

"And was it worth it, Azrael?" Eyes of the clearest blue, like ice chips lit from within, shone in Basil's face.

Rather than reply, because the answer was anything but clear, he said, "I've come to set you free."

"How magnanimous of you," was the dry reply.

"I am sorry it took so long."

For once, Daphne said nothing, but she did keep close, peeking around him. Not that her discretion mattered. Basil could smell life. The curse of the dead.

"How unlike you to bring me an apology." Basil neared, almost gliding in his robe. "It's been a long time since I've had human blood."

When she squeaked, he reached behind to reassure, not even understanding why. Since when did he care about a human's fear? Before his own incarceration, he'd brought more than a few willing and unwilling repasts for the undead man living below ground.

An old friend that, rather than kill, he'd imprisoned, reasoning some form of life was better than none. Having lived in confinement, he now knew better. Which was why he'd come. To give his friend the mercy he deserved.

Basil stopped just out of reach. "If the Shaitan roam once more, then why do you come here? You should be hunting them."

"As you said, it's been three thousand years since I promised to return. Your release is long overdue."

"You're not here to free me, are you?" Basil lowered his hood and canted his head, baring his neck. "Let's get this done. Kill me before I change my mind and decide this hellish existence is worth it."

Kill someone that used to be his friend until an unfortunate accident.

He put his hand on Basil's shoulder, their gazes meeting in understanding.

Only before he could act, a tiny woman inserted herself. "Hello, in case you didn't notice, you are both speaking in a language I don't understand. I've had enough of this. Who is this guy? Why does he live underground?"

It took him a moment to flip from his birth tongue to the English he'd learned. "This is Basil. A friend I owe a debt to."

"I thought you said he was dead." She eyed Basil. "Looks alive to me."

"Only because of the curse running through his body." At her curious stare, he explained. "Basil was infected with something and died, only to rise again with a taste for blood."

"So he's a vampire."

His turn to appear curious. "I do not know that word."

"Vampire, someone who was bitten or turned into the undead and who lives by sucking on the blood of others."

"You've heard of them. They exist in this time?"

"I don't know about exist, but there's been tons of stories told about them. Movies made. Books written." She shrugged. "They're considered quite romantic."

"You jest?" he scoffed. Only to have Basil exclaim in the language they shared, "What does the woman say?" Azrael explained.

Basil appeared intrigued. "Ask your woman, in these stories, these vampires, they lived above ground?"

He relayed the question, and she nodded. "Yes,

but at night, you know, because of the whole sun allergy thing."

It took only a moment to translate.

Basil glanced at him, and Azrael shook his head. "No. You know the rules." In his day, the undead were killed on sight. However, when it came to his close friend, he just couldn't bring himself to do it.

"Those who made the rules are long dead," Basil reminded.

"But they were created for a reason."

"To protect the fragile humans. I'm aware. But even this deep, I know they've multiplied. Can you really say that they're at risk given their numbers now?"

A good point. "Letting you leave this room means condemning some of those lives."

Basil shrugged. "Would you feel better if I said I'll only feed on the bad ones?"

Daphne tugged at his sleeve. "What's he saying?"

"He says if I free him he will feed only on the wicked."

"I'm cool with that," Daphne replied, drawing Azrael's ire. "Don't glare at me," she huffed. "Honestly, if your vampire friend is eating criminals, then that makes the world a better place, doesn't it?"

Despite not having the words translated, Basil grinned, knowing she took his side. Azrael could see the charming flirt who'd had all the girls falling at his feet. "Perhaps your lady friend can aid me in this new world."

Azrael bristled and, rather than admit a strange jealousy, stated, "I should speak to the others before making that kind of decision."

Basil's nostrils flared. "You want me to wait some more? And would you have wanted to wait if you knew freedom lurked within reach?"

He wished he could say he'd have taken the righteous path; however, after being imprisoned so long, he would have done anything to see the blue sky again. Even if released, Basil would never be able to bathe his face in the sun. But he could have a better existence than this.

Azrael glanced around the crypt. "I thought I was doing right by you."

"You locked me away and then disappeared. If it weren't for the wolves in the woods, I would have starved." The wild creatures were immune to the imprisoning magic. They could come and go, keeping Basil company—and fed.

"As you are aware, humans rule the world currently. They will notice if you murder them for food."

"I haven't waited this long for my freedom to be stupid," Basil spat.

"If you cause problems, I will come after you."

"Only if you survive your hopeless mission.

How much are you willing to sacrifice this time for a world that doesn't care?" Basil taunted.

A reminder that the path he'd set himself on ended only in two ways: death or further imprisonment.

I won't be locked away again.

He just couldn't.

And he also couldn't do it to Basil.

He moved to the entrance of the crypt and held out his hand. He couldn't pull on any magic in here, but he did have a weapon that could slice through the spells that layered this place.

The dagger marred the sigil, and he could practically feel the energy snap free. Over and over, the spells binding this place eased as each sigil was broken.

The final one was by the bottom step. And he paused before slicing it as well.

Whoosh. The spell hiding the tomb collapsed, and he half expected to see Basil rush past him.

Instead, that pale blue gaze stared back down the corridor. Basil took a step back then another.

Azrael frowned. "I thought you wanted freedom."

"I did, three thousand years ago. Lucky for me, someone helped me escape my prison well before you." As Basil spoke, Azrael could hear rustling. As of fabric.

When Basil emerged, he was dressed in modern

clothes. Denim. A collared shirt. The lenses he wore on his face dark.

"You've left the crypt?"

In perfect English, Basil stated, "For more than five hundred years now. Although, I will admit, the first century of that is a blur. Unlike you, I didn't have anyone else. I went mad for a while. But it passed."

"Why pretend?" Azrael asked.

"Because I was curious. Curious to see if you would kill me or let me go, or worse, condemn me again."

"You tricked me."

"And you honestly thought you should kill me. I'd say your infraction is greater."

"He's right," Daphne muttered.

"Be quiet," Azrael growled.

"Truth hurts," she coughed, shoving at her glasses.

"How fascinating. A female not impressed by your presence. And a human too. How that must gall." Basil smirked.

"If you knew I and the others were trapped, why did you not help us?"

Basil tilted his head. "Because I am not as nice as you."

His lips flattened. "I didn't come here to argue."

"You came for one of your precious seals."

"Where is it?"

"Long gone."

"Where?"

"I don't know, and I don't care. If you'll excuse me, I've other places I'd rather be." The man stepped past them but, before he left, turned to say one last thing. "Try not to martyr yourself for a world that wouldn't do the same for you."

And then Basil disappeared up the stairs.

"Fuck."

Daphne clucked. "Well, I'll bet that didn't go as you expected."

He shot her a dark look. "This isn't amusing."

"Never said it was. Ironic, though."

"We are leaving." His step might have had a slight stomp as he exited the crypt, but he made sure to not outpace the human. Daphne started out on her own two feet but soon lagged. He tossed her over a shoulder and ran despite her protests. Knew he neared the top when he heard the growls and howls as if a wolf pack had assembled.

Emerging, he was in time to see the last furry tail disappearing into the woods. When he glanced overhead, he couldn't help but see the vast winged shape that for a moment was silhouetted on the moon.

Daphne saw it, too, and said, "Is that a bat or dragon?

"A little bit of both."

"Now that you've taken care of that business, where to?"

Fatigue gripped him. And a need for safety. Not for him, but her while he rested. That meant there was only one answer. Which surprised him.

"Home."

Chapter Eleven

The fifth vow: Find and question Maalik about his lies.

Azrael knelt on scorched earth, watching as the last of the smoke sucked into the jewel. The moment there was none, he clipped a metal cage around it and uttered a word of magic. The dangerous amulet glowed and warmed before settling down. His fingers protected by gloves, he grabbed it by the thick linked chain, dangling it away from his body.

"I can't believe we did it." Nikail approached, too tired to swagger. "And we're sure that was the last one of them?"

"The last of any consequence. This is the seventh and final prison." Azrael dumped the amulet into a leather pouch then placed it inside a chainmail sack.

"Now we just need to hide it, and we'll be done. Finally.

It's been a long time coming." Nikail managed a grin through the grime coating his face.

"That was a hard-fought battle." Another man, sporting a trimmed beard and a gash through his shirt, which showed a flat stomach streaked with a red line, approached.

"Ridwan," Azrael said in salutation *"Did we all make it?"*

"Yeah. Maalik is puking though. The Shaitan managed to hit him with some kind of spell before we managed to contain it."

Azrael glanced down at the bag in his hand. *"Now that they're trapped, hopefully things can go back to normal."*

"Drinking, wenching, and doing very stupid things." Ridwan grinned.

"The stupidest," Nikail agreed. His face sobered. *"I can't believe we did it."*

"Don't celebrate yet." Maalik arrived, looking pale but determined.

"Why not? Once this is buried and forgotten, it's done. No more Shaitan, no more Iblis. We won," Ridwan insisted.

But the expression on Maalik's face... It didn't bode well.

Damn. A word that didn't truly convey what he felt in that moment.

Maalik appeared sick but determined. *"It is only a temporary victory. The Shaitan will return."*

"A problem for another generation," Ridwan declared. *"We did our part. Saved the world."*

"You only delayed the inevitable. Those prisons won't

hold them for forever. I saw it. Saw what happens when they return. Rivers of blood. Screams of the innocent." Maalik's eyes stared off, haunted by what he'd seen. Not the first vision he'd suffered.

"How long before they escape?" Ridwan asked.

"Not for a while," Maalik admitted.

"Meaning we might be long gone. Someone else will have to fight them," Nikail pointed out.

Maalik shook his head. "The generation that will eventually face the Shaitan will fail without our help. They won't have magic."

"How can they have no magic?" Azrael exclaimed, finally interjecting himself.

"The world moves on. Some things go extinct. When the Shaitan return, no one will know how to stop them."

"Meaning the Iblis will come." Nikail ducked his head. "All we've done is for nothing. We've only delayed the destruction."

"There is a way to ensure that doesn't happen," Maalik said.

Azrael stiffened "You've got a plan?"

Maalik nodded. "There is a way to ensure there are people to fight the Shaitan and teach a future generation how to use magic. All we have to do is bind ourselves to the spell holding the Shaitan in their prisons."

"Bind ourselves how?" asked Ridwan.

"With magic. My vision showed me how."

"Wouldn't it have been more useful for your vision to show you how to kill the Shaitan rather than trap them?" was Ridwan's complaint. *"Why can't we rid ourselves of them now while we have them trapped?"* He grabbed the chainmail sack and shook it.

He had a point.

"I don't know how to get rid of them. All I know is that I've seen the future where we're not there to fight them. Maybe you can live the rest of your life knowing the world is doomed, but I can't," Maalik snapped, his eyes sparking.

Ridwan sighed. "I hate it when you make me want to be noble."

"How long are we talking?" Azrael asked. *Because it obviously wouldn't happen in a natural lifetime.*

"An exact timeframe wasn't clear."

Lie. Azrael heard it and eyed his friend. Maalik knew more than he was saying. Not good, he'd wager, and yet his friend thought it was necessary.

Azrael found himself saying, "Whatever it takes."

For some reason, Maalik appeared sad when Ridwan and Nikail readily volunteered, barely waiting a beat before declaring they were in.

"I knew I could count on you." Maalik knew just who to ask. Who he could guilt.

After all, honor was everything.

One by one, the thirteen most powerful mages volunteered and gathered at a nexus point for magic deep in the desert. They rode in their horses, saddlebags laden per Maalik's instructions. He'd told them to bring as much as they could, obviously ensuring they wouldn't be without in the future.

Azrael had brought his entire weapons collection and his

leathers. Others had wagons sitting on the outside of the spot they'd tethered the horses. Some of them didn't want to leave their hoards unguarded.

Maalik wore a robe, as did a few others, but Azrael kept to his leathers and had his stave strapped down his back. He was never without it.

Maalik held a locked box. Inside, nestled amidst so much padding an egg wouldn't even break, was the amulet.

It would be going with them since they required it to launch the spell, but that was all Azrael knew. Maalik would reveal nothing more. Would they be asleep until the Shaitan escaped? Hopefully in a comfortable bed, protected from danger. Would the spell move them forward in time until they were needed? In that case, it wouldn't be long. In the blink of an eye, he'd be in the future. What wonders would it hold? Already in this time he'd seen such progress. Roads that connected cities. Massive buildings built with cunning and yet still managing beauty. Ways of moving water that didn't require daily trips to wells with buckets.

"Ready?" Maalik drew their attention and began.

The spell to bind them to the Shaitan prisons itself wasn't as complex as expected. It involved twelve figures standing around a thirteenth who knelt in front of a box. Maalik placed his hand on it, and as they chanted, it glowed bright, as did the streamers of power coming from the other twelve. Like a spoked wheel, the magic converged and began to spin, a widening vortex radiating out from the box. It glowed bright enough they had to close their eyes. Even then

139

they could still see the spell, a swirling maelstrom with a glowing nucleus.

It spun faster and faster, the force of it lifting the twelve off the ground. Round and round. The spell took on a life of its own, reaching a crescendo before it stilled.

The mages hung in the air. Not just them but everything around them: horses, wagons, loose rocks.

Then they dropped.

Azrael braced for impact, but the sharp whinnies didn't bode well for their steeds. Before he could recover, the spell struck.

There wasn't a rumble to warn. The ground just collapsed, sinking into a widening hole.

Azrael's first instinct was to grab his magic. But the spell had sucked him dry. He'd need time to recover, meaning he plummeted. The sinkhole narrowed, a funneling slide of sand jumbled with bodies. He saw a few wide eyes, but no one yelled. Like Azrael they saved their breath as they tunneled into the Earth faster and faster.

Terrifying, and yet even scarier? Their chute branched, and some of those tumbling people went in different directions along with some horses, who'd gone beyond fear into frothing terror. Bound packages jostled for position too. Azrael tucked his arms around himself as the tunnel got narrower.

Panic set in. Would he fit? Would he die wedged in a hole, slowly suffocating? What went wrong with the spell?

And then the thing he feared most happened. He got stuck.

The tunnel narrowed enough he was caught around the

shoulders. Not a pleasant feeling. It wasn't helped by the fact he couldn't touch his magic.

There wasn't anything to be heard but his own ragged pants. The tight vise of rock rubbed against him. He shifted, and for a second, it felt tighter, but he noticed his legs had some room. He managed to brace his feet and shove. Skin scraped from his shoulders. He grunted as he pushed again. He managed to loosen the grip. Not that it did him much good. Was he supposed to climb all the way back up?

The ground around him rumbled, a deep shiver that didn't bode well. A trickle of fine sand peppered his face. He needed to move. His feet shoved for traction, and he heaved his body.

He wasn't quite stuck; he just had nowhere to go.

He ran out of time. The trickle of sand turned into a pummeling wave, shoving him down, past the tight spot, with skin left behind.

The moment he hit open space he knew it. Felt it a moment of shock as he hung, suspended in the air.

It didn't last. He plummeted. He only narrowly managed to avoid smashing and dying. He landed a little hard on his feet, his knees bending with impact, but still complaining. A slight shower of dirt followed.

He glanced overhead, and saw a stony ceiling comprised of hard-packed dirt and rock. No sign of a hole. No exit he could see.

He took stock of his situation. The first thing he noticed was he definitely wasn't sleeping. Had he been thrust into the future?

That didn't feel right. Not mention, where were his friends?

"Ellona. Maalik. Jeebrelle. Nikail." He called their names, one by one.

Only his own voice echoed back.

A rumble shook the cave. Hard enough that he dropped to the ground and braced one hand on it.

Things shook. Dust and dirt, even chinks of rock fell. He closed his eyes, waiting. It subsided eventually. The ground ceased shaking, and the dust settled. Silence fell and pressed upon his ringing ears.

He cautiously opened his eyes but could see nothing. His eyes were good, but not that good. He held out his hand and called his magic.

He couldn't even get a spark. The damned spell had drained him. He'd rest and recover.

Only no matter how many times he dozed off, he couldn't make light, the most basic of tricks. Once he realized his magic wasn't returning, panic clawed.

Just as he thought the situation couldn't get worse, something skittered across loose pebbles.

Chapter Twelve

The only character t-shirt she owned: Baby Yoda smiling

Daphne awoke suddenly, gasping for air, eyes wide. Fear filled her. Her heart pounded. In the darkness, she could almost imagine she was still dreaming. Still in that scary place.

She shifted and realized she wasn't sleeping in a normal bed. Not even close. A dim light let her see well enough that she felt safe sitting up and eyeballing her nest of cushions and blankets. Encircled by—

Was that a freaking arm?

Not just any arm. She gaped at the scales, the size, and breathed, "Dragon." She didn't have the same terror as the first time, mostly because this time they were on the ground and she could actually study it. The size of its body with its wings tucked tight. Its giant head and even bigger mouth. With lots of teeth.

Definitely not one of her cuter figurines at home. This was the real thing. And it could eat her in a single bite.

She held her breath in sudden terror, only to realize if it intended to use her as a snack, she'd already be dead. She told her anxiety to take a hike. This was a nerd girl's dream come true. A dragon she could study.

But first...she really had to pee. Did this cave have a bathroom? She scrambled out of her cushy nest onto a dusty floor, where she promptly fell over. She didn't go quietly.

Grunt. Oomph. "Ow." *Scuff.* "Ugh."

It was enough to wake the dragon.

She heard a rustle as it shifted. She took her time rolling over and peeking at the huge scaled mound.

The dragon, with smoky skin and curling horns on his head, appeared to be sleeping, body wrapped around the bed she'd woken in as if it held a pile of treasure. He was absolutely massive.

"Damn, you're big."

An eye opened, just a single ginormous orb, and it stared at her.

She wasn't sure how she felt about it. Was that a happy gaze or a shut-up-before-I-eat-you glare?

She crossed her legs, her urge to pee more insistent.

The other eye opened, and the dragon snuffed.

Because breathing hotly on her wasn't scary. She clenched tighter. Please don't let her wet her pants in front of him.

She began inching away. Surely there was a bucket, a private corner, somewhere?

She had to turn her glance from him to see where she was going. Which meant she missed the whole dragon turning into a man. His voice startled her.

"Where are you going?"

"Bathroom right here, right now, if you don't point me in the direction of a toilet." She cast him a quick glance to see him dressed.

A brow rose, and his lip tugged. "To your left you'll see an arch with a door in the wall."

Turning, she noticed it right away, across a room that made little sense to her. But her need took precedence. She almost ran for the door and pushed inside, only to stop in surprise. She'd walked into some kind of ancient bathroom. Or so it seemed. Carved from the very rock was a counter with a sink fed by a gurgling tube of water. A never-ending stream.

Even better, beside it was a carved seat with a hole in it.

As she went, she really hoped nothing hid in the

hole. Her imagination easily conjured a rat or something worse lunging for a bite.

She finished her business without dying and made her way back out to the larger cave—and a pacing Azrael.

As caves went, the one she was in appeared to have quite a few upgrades.

"Where are we?" she asked, craning to look.

"My home." He paused and pivoted to face her. "It was the only place I could think of that would provide protection."

"From whom? You think your vampire friend is coming after you?"

"He'd be within his right to try. I never meant to leave him imprisoned that long. Circumstances intervened."

She'd gotten that gist when they finally spoke in English. What she did wonder was, "How long did you leave him in that crypt?"

"Three thousand years."

The number boggled her mind. She tried to make sense of it. "Wait a second, you're three thousand years old."

"More or less."

"You don't look more than thirty."

"Because the spell that kept us locked in the caves prevented aging."

Slowly she made sense of what he was saying and realized her dream might not be a dream after all. "Hold on, you mean you lived *here* for three thousand years?"

"More or less," was his cryptic reply. "I did move around periodically. There are tunnels and other caverns."

"And you built this?" she asked, waving a hand at the etched frescoes on the stone walls.

"Wasn't much else to do during my imprisonment."

She had to know if what she'd experienced while dreaming was true. "It wasn't supposed to be a prison. You volunteered."

That brought an angry tug to his mouth. "I wouldn't have if I'd known what it meant."

"I don't believe you. I think you still would have because you're a hero." The statement slipped from her lips, and for a moment, he appeared shocked.

"I am not a hero."

"But you are a survivor. One of thirteen."

He eyed her suspiciously. "How do you know?"

"Because I saw it in my dream. There were thirteen of you, and a box. About this big." She held out her hands. "With a necklace inside. You guys cast some kind of spell and got sucked into the Earth."

His eyes widened. "You had a vision."

"I guess. It seemed so real." She frowned. "Was it real?"

"I'd have to know the entirety of what you saw to verify."

So she told him, and Azrael said nothing as she recited what she remembered. But his expression, stony and stoic, let her know she'd seen the truth.

"I can't believe that happened to you," she finished with a scrunch of her nose.

"I wish I could forget." As if surprised by his admission, he turned away.

"I saw thirteen in the dream, but only four of you emerged from the desert, according to the news. Did you all live in the caves?"

"Yes."

"So you weren't alone?"

"Yes and no. I spent periods being companionable. Other times, I needed to get away," he muttered.

"That must have sucked." When he frowned deeper, she explained. "I mean, that probably wasn't fun for you. I'm sorry. I'll stop talking about it."

"Why are you interested?"

"Because." How to explain her fascination with his tragic backstory?

He glanced at her. "That's not an answer."

Her turn to offer an enigmatic smile. "Can you blame me? You're like nobody I've ever met. And I'm not just talking about the dragon part. I want to know more about you. How did you survive? Did you eat? How about boredom?"

Azrael snorted. "Not much more to tell. I spent an eternity exploring the limited warren of tunnels connecting me to twelve other people."

"How big are we talking?" she asked.

"I know not the exact measurement, other than it seemed huge for the first century. But over time, as you run into the same things over and over..." He paused, and she thought he was done until he said, "After awhile, it's enough to make a person lose their mind. To do things they never imagined."

"You survived."

"Did I? Look at me, returning to my prison because it feels safe." He snorted.

"Nothing wrong with turning to the familiar. And it doesn't seem like it's a prison anymore. You can come and go as you please."

"For now."

"You're worried about another spell locking you back in."

He shrugged. "I was at first, until I realized there are too few left to cast it. Then there is the fact magic has been almost eradicated by technology."

"Which is why the world needs you. You're the one who knows how to get rid of those Shaitan things." She remembered his friend's claim in the dream.

He scowled. "I don't know how to kill them. The best we could do last time was contain them."

"So we bottle them again. Three thousand years is a long time to find a solution."

"It won't be so easy. I cannot do it alone." A grim admission that had him clenching his fists.

"What about your three other friends?"

He shook his head. "Only Jeebrelle might help. Israfil and Nikail have chosen to abstain."

"I'll help."

She expected his snort of derision. "Help how?"

"I don't know yet, but I can start by doing some research to see if there is a modern solution to genies. I don't suppose you stocked the place with a laptop and internet?"

He rolled his shoulders and rocked on his heels. "No. As you might have noticed, my home isn't exactly luxurious. Since my release, I haven't had much time to replenish."

"I'd say you did pretty good given what you started with." She could only imagine the raw look of the cavern when he arrived. As she craned to look around, she could see the transformation. The place was a veritable work of art. Almost everything was carved. The exceptions being a highly polished counter and a jagged piece of glass framed against a wall.

"I had to be innovative."

"You're being modest. Living here had to be

hard. Especially since there's no windows." She glanced overhead, and this time realized there were walkways spun of a fine filament and climbing the walls in delicate steps before ringing it.

"No windows or door. We are much too far below the surface, in a place where time moves differently."

At the reminder, her heart stopped. "If I'm underground, how do I get out?"

"You don't. Not until I have to go somewhere and take you with me."

"Meaning I'm your prisoner." She hugged herself. So much for that brief moment of connection. He'd just reminded her of why he'd kidnapped her.

"More like a temporary guide through this new world."

"A guide? What kind of guide? Where? Can you be a little more specific? Because, while I know the city kind of well, I'm not too good navigating outside of it."

His lips pressed into a thin line and his fists clenched before he relented enough to say, "It is not actual directions I require but assistance in understanding how things work now. Things like those boxes that contact people far away. Passing for a modern human without drawing notice."

"How about you start by not calling us human with such a sneer?"

He stared at her. "And that is exactly why it has to be you. You're not intimidated by me."

"You mean on account of the whole dragon thing?" She rolled a shoulder. "I'm not one to put something on a pedestal that easily. People do that too much with celebrities. I'd like to think I'm a little more discerning."

"In my day—"

She interrupted him. "I get it, in your day you walked twenty miles to fetch water, made your women stay home and have babies, and acted like veritable asses. But guess what, this is the twenty-first century. Things have changed. Women have rights. We are equals." She held herself ramrod straight.

"Why wouldn't you be?" He sounded genuinely confused. "My kind has never had the sexist separation that plagues the humans and other races. Strength of magic is the key element."

"What about compassion and wisdom?"

"Can only be applied if you have the strength to force it."

"Dude. That's not how you rule. You should rule with fair laws and justice for all. Where the strong help the weak."

"And I begin to see the problem with this time period." He shook his head. "The Shaitan won't care about your laws. They only understand force."

"We can fight if we have to."

"With guns?" He arched a brow. "They will turn to smoke and never suffer a wound."

"We'll pull a Ghostbuster on them and suck them into a containment unit."

"They have magic. Without spells, they'll escape."

She frowned. "The dream I had said you'd vanquish them when you returned."

"Maalik predicted that. Yes."

"I hear a 'but.'"

"If that was true, then why did Maalik disappear? You would think the person who predicted our victory would have remained to play a part of it, especially given the decimation in our ranks."

"How did your friends die?" It was a morbid question, and yet the desire to know proved strong.

"Not all at once, if that's what you're wondering. We began as eight men, five women in a confined space with limited entertainment and supplies. Add in a long time waiting." He rolled his big shoulders. "Some deaths were accidents. Some weren't."

"I thought you were immortal."

"Not exactly. We don't age, like normal people would. But we can be killed."

A demigod, in other words. Why did he have to get more interesting with every word uttered? "You said before you wouldn't have agreed if you'd known how long you'd be imprisoned."

He glanced at her. Pressed his lips tight. "Would you?"

"I don't know."

"Let me answer for you. Being immortal isn't a gift, but a curse."

"In other words, you regret your decision."

"Regret, yes, and at the same time, I would still make the same choice," he said in a weary voice.

"Because you're a hero," she softly stated. A sexy one who could have stepped out of the pages of a book.

"Fuck." He grimaced. "Hardly a hero."

His denial only made him sexier.

"Really? So you're not going to try and save the world from the Shaitan?"

He glared.

She smiled. "At the museum, you said something about seven seals. If two are broken, then we need to locate the other five bottles and protect them."

"Not all of them are bottles. Only four are amphora. There are also two rings and an amulet."

"Which, if destroyed, will open a gate to the netherworld, releasing a monster. Got it." And her mother said reading all those dungeon and dragon books as a teen wouldn't come in useful. Now that she'd accepted this was really happening, it wasn't hard to grasp what had to be done. "Finding those seals is only part of the problem. The true task is getting rid of the genies."

"The Shaitan." He tucked his hands behind his back and glanced upward at stalactites that dripped to join the stalagmites on the floor, all of them carved into columns, telling a story.

But how much of it was real? That giant spider looming over the man with the spear was probably an exaggeration. Right?

"Surely they have a weakness. Something that can kill them."

He shook his head. "You think we didn't try? They are tricky, which was why we had to trap them when we couldn't find a way to destroy them."

"Seven seals. Does that mean seven Shaitan?"

"Seven servants of the Iblis. If they were to ever combine their strength, they could rip open a portal to Hades."

"Because of course Hell exists."

His brows rose. "You've heard of Hell, but didn't know of dragons? In my day, humans worshipped us."

"In my day, dragons have a thing for virgins and make billions at the box office."

He blinked. "Why would we want virgins? They cry."

"Speaking from experience?" she declared hotly. She couldn't have said why she was miffed.

His lip quirked at the corner. "No, but I have friends who were fond of seducing the innocent."

"That is seriously messed up." Then she blurted out, "Are you married?"

"I was a captive."

"And? There were twelve other people. Surely you hooked up."

"Others did. Not me."

"Didn't you miss it?" She didn't have a super active sex life, but even she needed the touch of another.

"I kept busy."

"And must have switched hands often or you'd have one super-strong right-handed grip," she muttered.

His lips twitched. Of course he understood the dirty joke.

"What part of the legends are true? Dragons obviously fly. What about breathing fire?"

"That is a red trait."

"There are colors?"

"Yes. The colors determine the types of abilities the dragons have."

"What's your special power?" she asked.

"I'm a mage."

"Meaning what? You toss fireballs. Bring brooms to life. Pull bunnies out of your hat?"

He blinked. "Is the world truly that oblivious to what magic can do?"

The remark lifted her shoulders. "Until I met you, I was under the impression magic wasn't real."

"The ignorance of this time is staggering."

"Then I guess you'll need to educate me," she sassed. "Is it true dragons love gold and jewels?"

"Some do. Others have different concepts of what makes a treasure."

"Such as? What did you used to collect?"

"Nothing."

"You don't have a hoard?" she queried.

"I used to, but I lost it a long time ago." The poor guy sounded sad.

"I guess you couldn't bring it with you when you got sucked into the cave. What was it?"

He shook his head. "You wouldn't think it was a very interesting collection."

"You are not going to tell me what it was."

"No."

For some reason it only made her more determined to find out.

"How long are we staying here?"

"I don't know." He raked a hand through his hair. "This modern world is hard to navigate. There is so much noise everywhere it makes the Shaitan hard to locate."

"They'll go to where the treasures are hidden." It seemed obvious to her.

"Obviously."

"So, we get there first and lay a trap for when the genie comes."

He shook his head. "No. Traveling to the seals will only reveal their location."

She couldn't have said what rang false, but in a moment of insight, she said, "You don't know where they are, do you?"

He fidgeted. Big bad dragon looked sheepish as he admitted, "A lot has changed. When we originally hid them, we didn't expect to be gone so long. The seals have disappeared."

"Can't you cast a spell to find them?"

He shook his head. "They're invisible to all forms of detection. It was the best way to hide them and not draw attention if they were accidentally discovered."

"I thought you said they hummed."

"When I got near enough, I could sense it, but not before."

"Then how did you find it?" How had he known to come to the museum?

"I saw a picture of the amphora. I made haste to its last known location."

"Okay, so that makes things more difficult. At least you know where the amulet is. I saw it in my dream. It went with you."

"It went missing over a thousand years ago."

"Well fuck," she muttered, drawing a surprised look from him.

He smiled. "Do you know I waited three thousand years to find that word? None of the languages I spoke had anything so versatile in my time."

"It's a good word."

"The best," he agreed. For a moment he was silent. "A lot has changed."

"Especially in the last one hundred years. Industrialization exploded."

"Humans have evolved too. You're not as naïve as before."

"You mean not bowing down to your dragon and having minds of our own?" She smiled sweetly. "It's called equality."

"Like I said, things have changed. Which is damned annoying."

"Well, you've got me now to help you figure things out." Funny how she was coming around to the idea.

"I don't know if that's going to work." He rubbed his face.

"Why?"

"You're too attractive."

A compliment and yet he made it sound like a complaint. "That's a problem?"

"Yes, it's a problem. You're a distraction I don't have time for."

"Me?" The very idea she could throw him off his game was ridiculous. And sexy.

"You've been preying on my mind since the

moment we met," he growled, stalking toward her. "If I didn't know better, I'd think you cast a spell on me."

"I'm not a witch."

"Perhaps not, but you certainly are a seductress." He stopped in front of her, a looming presence.

She stared at him, licking her lips, at a loss for words, wishing he'd kiss her. Awareness flickered between them.

"I can't resist," he muttered before he yanked her hard against his chest, startling her.

Before she could suck in a breath, his mouth was on hers, devouring and sucking, the passion almost furious in its nature. She clung to his lips as desperately, consumed by the same ferocious desire.

When he finally let her breathe, it took her a moment. She eventually managed to gaze at him with heavy-lidded eyes. "I thought you didn't want to kiss me."

His expression smoldered. "Don't ever think I don't want to kiss you. The problem is stopping."

"Why stop?"

He vibrated and slowly his head dipped, but just before he would have touched his mouth to hers—

"Azrael, why didn't you send word we had guests?"

Chapter Thirteen

Sixth vow made right then and there: Kill Nikail.

A zrael would have gladly throttled Nikail. As usual, his timing proved most annoying.

"Nick," he acknowledged. Perhaps not his brother by blood but definitely a sibling by shared experience, Nikail was one of the four who'd survived their prison. Physically at least. His mind though....

"How nice you've finally decided to take a bit of time to yourself."

A dig that caused him to growl, "I haven't forgotten my task."

"Really?" Nikail eyed her. "Does she have a seal inside her mouth that only your tongue can retrieve?"

It had been a long time since embarrassment

heated his skin. "Daphne was there when the second amphora was broken."

"And? What possible use can you have for a *human*?" Nick eyed her coldly.

"Excuse me, but I'm standing right here. Show a little respect," Daphne snapped.

"It speaks. Without being told." Nikail sneered. "A shining example of what we sacrificed for. Ungrateful humans who don't know to keep their mouths shut when in the presence of their superiors."

"Wow, three thousand years and still a dick."

Nikail's eyes narrowed. "Are you trying to die?"

Azrael stood between them before he had to act. "Was there a particular reason for your visit?"

"Some of us have been working. Researching."

"I thought you weren't interested in helping."

"I'm not. But some habits are hard to break," grumbled Nikail.

"What did you discover?"

Nikail eyed Daphne and said nothing.

"You can speak in front of her. She is an attendant for the reliquaries of priceless artifacts."

Nick eyed her up and down. "In my day, they had to have a certain level of fitness to guard magic. Then again, what can you expect from a world that exiled all its mages."

"What do you mean all?" Azrael scoffed. "That's impossible."

"You'd think, and yet it happened. Not right after our departure. It was a slow descent as the Septs devolved into spatting groups that decimated each other, making it easy for the humans to eventually hunt our kind almost to extinction."

"Humans killing dragons? But how?" he exclaimed, only to glance down at his sheath. There was one metal deadly to dragons. Dracinore. It made them mundane. Unable to shift.

Nick confirmed it. "The humans were given Dracinore. Loads of it, smuggled into the world by mages. Our mages."

"No." Azrael shook his head. In his day, there were only a few rules the mages followed, and one of them was bring no harm to dragons.

"If the sparse histories I've found can be believed, our magical brethren planned a coup with the humans, only to be betrayed. The Septs were hunted to almost extinction. Apparently, they only barely survived, but the resentment ran hot. All the mages, even those that weren't to blame, got exiled to another dimension."

"That explains why we are needed. The Septs got rid of magic." He paced. "What else have you learned?"

"Not much, other than they recently united under a golden king. The first in generations apparently, with a brother who is the first mage to be born since the exile."

His lips pursed. "There are no others?

Nikail shook his head. "None, which I guess means the end after all."

"What's he talking about?" Daphne asked.

It was Nikail who chose to bluntly explain. "What that means is we sacrificed our lives for nothing. There aren't enough mages in the world to put those that have escaped back inside a cage, so why bother risking my life?"

Azrael pursed his lips. "If we do nothing, there won't be a world for us to live in."

"Then better enjoy it while we can."

Daphne stepped forward. "How about we stop with the pessimism and come up with a plan?"

"And what kind of plan would you suggest?" Nikail mocked. "Even if we could place the Shaitan back in their prison, it won't last forever. I am certainly not volunteering to go back to my prison. What about you, Azrael?"

"No."

"Exactly. Now, you can do as you like, but as for me, I'm going to enjoy every moment I have left. I hear the Bahamas are very nice." Nick left as abruptly as he'd arrived, and Azrael couldn't help but sigh.

"Fuck." He'd be saying it a lot more before the end was nigh.

She put a hand on his arm. "You can't give up. There must be a way to stop the Shaitan."

"I don't see how. Nikail is correct. It took thirteen of the strongest dragon mages to lock them away last time."

"Which is why we'll destroy them instead."

He side-eyed her. "Because we didn't try that in the past."

"But you only tried using magic. Right?"

"What else would we use?"

"That stuff you and Nikail were talking about."

"Dracinore?" He took on a pensive expression. As he recalled, the Shaitan dissolved before the metal could strike its flesh. "Even if it did harm them, there is not enough of it."

Was there? He didn't actually know. In his day, the dangerous metal was tossed into volcanoes to destroy it. He couldn't believe anyone, especially mages, would dare smuggle Dracinore into the world, but the dagger by his side said otherwise. There had to be more. Perhaps even a weapon that would kill the Shaitan.

"We should get your knife to a lab and figure out what it's made of."

He gazed at her blankly. "I don't understand."

"A lab—short for laboratory—is a place where scientists examine things down to a molecular level."

He waited. Patiently.

She fidgeted. "Er. They deconstruct stuff to figure out how it's made and how it works."

"Science," he said slowly. Not a thing completely unheard of in his time, however a being that could do magic had little time for those kinds of studies.

"Don't knock it. Humans have made some pretty incredible stuff."

"Like capturing images and playing them on strange devices."

"Dude, that's just the tip of the iceberg. We've made weapons, too, stuff that makes guns look like toys."

He eyed her. "Is it true you've created a bomb that destroys entire cities and leaves everything poisoned?"

"Yeah. We're good at killing things." She rolled her shoulders as if in apology.

He grinned. "Don't be sorry. You've just given me hope. We shall take the dagger to a laboratory."

"Which is part one of the plan. The second part might be a little more complicated. We should also get a sample of a Shaitan to have it analyzed."

"Pieces will be difficult. The Shaitan do not bleed and are too strong to easily capture and contain." Azrael didn't recall many instances where they'd actually harmed the Shaitan. Harried and disrupted, yes, but splitting them into smaller pieces? It could be done, but the Shaitan always recovered, and the piece they cut off became one of the lesser jinn.

"Hard or not, we need something we can dissect. How else will we find a weakness?"

He rubbed his chin. "The Shaitan cannot realize what we are doing. For this sample you seek, we can use their brethren, the Ifrit. They are weak versions." Who stayed away from dragons.

"Do you know where to find one?"

"No. But I know a place we can look." He'd come across traces of an Ifrit recently on his travels. The tiny town he'd been born into had grown to a sprawling mess of a city.

Given he'd recovered from his last magical expenditure, Azrael was ready to act. He lifted a hand and pulled magic to sketch a portal. As it began to rip the air open, he glanced at Daphne. She was disheveled, her hair a mess. Her orange attire was filthy and in need of washing. He'd used magic to keep himself fairly fresh. She didn't have the same ability. He'd spent so long in his own company he'd forgotten simple manners.

"But before we embark on our next quest, we will refresh ourselves."

A hopeful expression appeared. "Please, please tell me that means a shower and clean clothes?"

"How do you feel about a bath?"

The squeal was an adequate and loud answer. "Where is it?"

"Follow me."

She started out sticking close to Azrael but

quickly became distracted by the carvings on the wall. He'd spent the better part of three centuries decorating the space.

She pointed. "Did any of those scenes actually happen?"

He glanced over at the worm, giant and hungry. Not as hungry as him. "Not for a long time."

"And that?"

The spider infestation. That had been rather unpleasant. He nodded.

"Fun place," she muttered.

They went through a passage, also intricately decorated, with a niche running the entire length filled with statues, all of them meticulously carved by hand. She ran her fingers over a few and stopped in front of a rock carved into a hunched body holding its head in its hands.

"You weren't kidding when you said you kept busy." She said it in a sad tone. Glanced at him.

"It is when your mind strays that the problems start. If you give it a task, something that has to be done, a focus, then time passes somewhat more quietly."

"You have a talent."

"You say that only because you didn't see my early work. I was terrible for almost a century, but I eventually improved and redid my practice etchings."

They exited the tunnel into a room that was

basically a lake edged in a ring of stone that he'd carved to appear like shells, interlocked and leading into a basin. He'd held his breath and chiseled, piece by piece, the underwater creatures and detail.

The stalactites hanging overhead had a natural glow, and a fling of magic ignited the glitter, illuminating the water.

"That's not a bath, it's a swimming pool," she exclaimed.

"The water is pleasantly warm."

"Really?" She dipped a toe and grinned, her face beaming. "I can't wait to get wet."

Her enthusiasm fired his own. It would be nice to rid himself of clothing and be naked. As a dragon, it was natural to not wear adornment, but as a human...all those fleshy dangly bits looked odd uncovered.

Azrael stripped, dropping his clothes onto a stool that rose from the floor, a former stalagmite repurposed. He'd have to give his leathers a good cleaning, although it could wait. Since his release from his prison, the one thing he had done was replenish his wardrobe. The first time he'd teleported in he'd brought an armful of things just in case his freedom was temporary.

He'd visited a few times since, stocking the place, not willing to admit a fear he'd be imprisoned again. He'd brought soil and seeds, fabric by the bolts, and books. So many, many books.

As he entered the water, the heat easing his muscles, a sigh left him. It had been awhile since he'd exerted enough to enjoy the simple things like a bath. As he stepped down into the deeper part of the pool, he realized he didn't hear her splashing. A glance over his shoulder showed her standing, fully clothed, on the edge.

"Are you not cleansing?" he asked from the last step before the pool turned bottomless. He didn't know how far it went, only that he couldn't hold his breath long enough to find an exit. And every so often, something big rose from the deep. Good thing he'd not mentioned it given her trepidation.

"You mean have a bath at the same time as you?"

He glanced around at the massive stone tub more than thirty feet across and twice as wide. "I'm fairly confident we have enough room to share."

"Promise to not peek."

The request, meant to preserve her modesty, surprised him enough he laughed out loud.

"What's so funny?" she huffed.

"That you think I am interested in your nudity."

"Well, gee, thanks. That makes me feel just great," was her sour reply. She'd taken it as a criticism.

"You misunderstand. Dragons do not have the same issues with nudity as humans. You were always the type to cover up and treat the body as a sexual and, at the same time, shameful thing. To us, skin is skin."

"If you're not attracted to bodies, then what does turn you on?" she asked, the rustle of clothes indicating she shed them.

"Scent. Personality." He didn't mention just plain need. It had been a long time since he'd desired anyone. He thought himself past that kind of thing until very recently.

Like since a certain night at a museum. He glanced to the side as he heard the splash of water. Saw Daphne stepping gingerly into the water. Naked. Beautiful.

He noticed every single curve. The indent of her waist. Flare of her hip. Swell of her breasts. The pink in her cheeks. The shocked, "Azrael! You said you wouldn't look."

He'd also said he wasn't interested in her naked body, and yet the sight of her affected him. The water hid the swelling of his cock.

Soon it also hid her body as she submerged to her neck. "Oh, this is nice."

She dunked her head underwater for a moment before rising and flipping her hair. The wet drops hit him in the face.

She laughed. "Oops. Guess this pool isn't big enough for the two of us."

"Don't worry, I know how to share." He slapped the water with a hand and repaid the kindness.

She only laughed harder and dove away, twisting in the water. Within a second, he was after her, chasing and grabbing her ankle. Giving it a yank. Making her blow bubbles underwater.

She turned and dove on him, but rather than wrestle, her fingers dug for his ribs, and for the first time since he was a boy, he remembered what it was like to be tickled.

His turn to blow bubbles.

They kicked to the surface, rising at the same time, wet faces only inches apart. Treading water. Huffing for air.

Their gazes met.

He drew her close. Held her tight. Let his magic float them that he might kiss her. And kiss her deeply.

She replied softly at first, as if shy. Hesitant.

He whispered, "Should I stop?"

"No. Never." She wrapped her arms around him and meshed their lips. Her legs wrapped around him, and he would have sunk with her if not for the magic he wrapped around them to keep them afloat.

He cupped her bottom, growling into her mouth at the feel of her. It had been so long. He wanted more than anything to taste her, which was why he floated them to the stairs and sat her high enough that her breasts were exposed to him. Before he explored, he kissed her, a slow exploration that left her breathless and gyrating against him.

He cupped her head and tilted it, letting his lips move from her mouth and across her jawline before nipping the tip of her earlobe. She made a sound that was half growl, half mewl. It did things to him. Made him throb with need. He wanted to be impatient and go right for the personal pleasure. Sate himself. But that would be over too quickly.

He needed this to last. To make her cry out in pleasure first.

Given she sat in water, he could float into the position he wanted, hands gripping the stairs to put his mouth level with her breasts. Perfect globes. He brushed his mouth across her nipples, and her head angled back.

He stroked over it again, feeling it pucker at his touch. He gripped it with his lips. Took the peak into his mouth. Sucked.

She cried out and grabbed at his head. Encouragement to do it again. So he tugged that nipple. Sucked it. Nipped it. Switched sides and sucked some more as she gasped and clung to his bare shoulders. He thrust a hand between her thighs and cupped her. Would swear he felt her pulsing against his palm.

He lifted her a few more steps until she sat on the edge, and when she parted her legs…

He saw trust. Desire. And he felt heat.

Her heat and he wanted to bask in it.

His lips touched the skin of her inner thigh.

She shivered.

He kissed the other side before rubbing his bristled jaw against the sensitive skin.

She moaned.

He teased his way up both her legs until he finally kissed the prize.

She arched, her hips bucking, her fingers digging against stone. His mouth blew hotly on her, and she quivered.

The heat of her increased. She trembled and made noises. Sweet noises.

He inserted a finger and felt her clench him. A second finger and her hips rocked against his hand as he licked.

She came suddenly, with a sharp cry and a spasm of muscles that had him swelling in satisfaction.

But he wasn't done. He kept working her until she began to tense again, her body not quite done. Only when she was gasping and rolling against him did he move to cover her, his bigger frame dwarfing her.

She smiled up at him. Put her arms around his neck and drew him down for a kiss while he teased her between the legs. Played with her until she writhed and begged him.

"Azrael. I need you."

Magic words that had him sliding between her thighs, his length hard and ready. He pressed against her, and her body opened for him. He slid in, feeling her tense and hot all around. A perfect fit. And then she flexed. Squeezed him so tight he gasped.

"Are you okay?" she asked, worried about him.

"Never better." He'd found nirvana, and as he rocked, that pleasure increased, grew and grew until it burst into something beyond ecstasy.

For a moment, he was nothing and everything, and he wasn't alone.

Even when he returned to his body, he wasn't alone. He held her, and she held him.

After three thousand years…he'd finally found a mate.

Chapter Fourteen

Next shirt she planned to buy: Save a horse,
ride a dragon.

Azrael emerged from the tunnel, his stave slung over his
shoulder and strung with a single skinny rat, to find
Maalik waiting for him. It had been a century since they'd
spoken. Maybe longer. He still had a hard time forgiving him
for the lies that stole their freedom. In that time, Maal had
acquired a wild gleam in his eye.

"Hello, Maal. What brings you for a visit?" Because
during their last encounter, Maalik made it clear he wanted
some alone time.

"I'm here to say goodbye."

Those words froze Azrael. "You can't kill yourself. You're
the reason we're here."

Maalik's lips turned down. "I've played my part. My
future is down a different branch."

"And how are you getting there? There is no exit. No tunnel large enough to take us past the edges of the spell." With magic, they could have escaped. Three of them knew how to create a rift and shorten the distance it took to travel. But for that they needed magic, and this place had none.

"Don't worry about me. You're the one who's going to have the most difficult task. The only one to truly believe in what we're doing."

"I can't do this alone."

"You won't be." Maalik winked. *"Tell her hello from me."*

"Tell who?"

"No time to explain. I've already said too much. I have to go."

"Go where?" Azrael asked, just as his friend jumped into his pool. He'd only just finished the far edge and still had underwater to carve.

Maalik floated to the surface and treaded water. *"One day, if the fates allow, and I follow the right branch, we'll meet again."*

Before Azrael could retort, something rose from the deep, too fast to react or cry out a warning.

His mouth only had time to open and Maalik was gone, yanked under and down. Out of sight in the amount of time it took for him to say, *"Damn."*

Daphne awoke, startled and sweating, with Azrael over her.

"Wake up, you're yelling in your sleep."

She stared at him. "I saw you. Again. In my dream."

"Seemed more like a nightmare."

"Because it was scary," she said with a frown. "I saw your friend getting yanked by some tentacle. It came up from the bottom of the pool." Her eyes widened. "Holy shit, we swam in that pool. We could have died."

"Ah, you saw the day Maal disappeared." Azrael rolled until he lay beside her in the nest of pillows. He'd insisted they sleep before heading off again. Although that sleep only happened after a big meal he popped out to fetch—which meant fifteen minutes of panic—then slow lovemaking that finished with a snuggle.

"A monster dragged him down. I saw it. And you took me swimming in that bottomless lake!" she accused, jabbing a finger in his rock-hard chest.

"That was the only time I ever saw that creature. And Maal obviously knew it was coming, or he wouldn't have jumped in."

"Why am I dreaming your memories?" she asked.

"I don't know."

"How do I stop it?"

He rolled his shoulders. "Given I am at a loss to explain why you're reliving key moments in my life, I don't think I can help."

"There has to be a reason this is happening.

Maybe I'm supposed to figure something out and these dreams are clues."

He arched a brow. "Or you're dreaming of me because of your intense fascination with me. Which is normal given my evident splendor."

"What you are is arrogant." She shoved at him. "Be serious. These dreams are weird. If they were sex dreams, then wouldn't I be in them? Thing is, I'm not. They're all about you. About your fight with the Shaitan."

"Except for the one that just woke you. That had everything to do with Maalik and no one else."

"Are you sure about that?" She tapped her lower lip. "He was the one originally in charge of the amulet."

"But he didn't have it when it disappeared."

"Are you sure he didn't?"

He shrugged. "Could be he had the seventh seal and lied, but if that's the case, it disappeared with him. Wherever it went, I don't think it can return."

"You hope. Just like you hope that thing that took your friend never comes back while you're having a bath." She shivered. "I don't know if I'll ever be able to get in it again." Which implied she'd be sticking around. But he didn't remark on it.

"The pool isn't dangerous. Not anymore. A few hundred years of culling got rid of the things that liked to try and kill me."

"How can anything kill you if you're immortal?" She was half perched atop him, still naked, and loving the feel of her skin on his.

"Because while long lived, we are still flesh and bone. While in this cavern network, which Dina declared to be at the core of the earth, the aging process is simply stopped. But we can still die."

"Does this mean when you leave your cave you start getting old?"

"Not right away. There is a residual effect that takes some time to fade when above ground."

"You can feel yourself getting older?" she asked.

He nodded.

She glanced around. "Does this mean I don't get old when I'm in here?"

"I don't know. I've never brought a human here before."

She took a second to absorb before smiling. "Glad I'm your first." She rolled out of his nest and headed to the wall and a bookshelf. Naked. Ass wiggling.

She held in a grin as she heard him following. Nice to know he liked what he saw.

She stopped in front of the books, old and leather bound, in a language she didn't understand. She traced her finger over the spines. "What are these?"

"Journals."

She slid out a tome and opened it, frowning at the strange sheets bound inside. "It's not paper."

"Pounded eel skin."

She didn't drop it but put it back on the shelf.

"You won't find anything interesting in them."

She turned to find him right behind her, his arms reaching to bracket her.

"You wrote them. And I find you fascinating," she admitted.

He dropped a kiss on her lips. "A feeling reciprocated, but it will have to wait. We have a jinn to trap."

She glanced down at herself. "I might be a tad underdressed for outside the cave."

The corner of his lip lifted. "Personally, I like you naked, but I don't know if I want to share that particular delight with anyone. Let us see what kind of attire we can manage."

It turned out he didn't have much that fit a woman. At all. The best she managed was a shirt that hung mid-thigh. "We need to go to my apartment first. Can you portal us there?" she asked.

"Yes. But it will deplete my magical stores. It is a waste of a trip."

"To you maybe, but I'd like to have some clothes that fit and shoes that are broken in. Not to mention, I have a computer we can use for research. And the phone number of the guy I know at a lab who can get started on that dagger."

"A human?"

"What did you expect? It's not as if I know any

dragons we can ask for help." Which wasn't exactly true. "Or we could try and contact Babette."

"You cannot trust a silver." He shook his head.

"What is that supposed to even mean?"

"In my time, they were weak and conniving."

"Three thousand years, dude. People change."

He appeared obstinate. Ready to argue some more, only to exhale loudly and say, "Fine. We shall fetch you some attire then contact the silver."

"Was that so hard?"

He dragged her close and planted a fervent kiss on her lips. "Very."

Their departure was delayed a few minutes as they took care of that problem.

When it was time to leave, she could practically see him gathering the magic to open the doorway and put her to sleep.

"Leave me awake," she begged.

"I don't dare," was his reply. "There are things in the nothing place. Whispers that might drive you mad if you heard them."

"Isn't it dangerous for you?"

"I'm not easily swayed." He smiled and winked. "How about I promise to wake you the moment we reach the other side?"

She nodded and tucked herself against him. He kissed her temple, and her eyes fluttered shut. When they opened again, she was on a rooftop with an aluminum spinning chimney.

"Is this my building?" she asked. She'd never thought to visit the rooftop before. "How do we get inside?"

When he did his imitation of a certain super-hero, and basically climbed down the wall in defiance of gravity with her clinging to him like a monkey, she almost wished he'd left her asleep. They climbed through her bedroom window, where she stood, hands on her hips, shaking her head at him.

"You know, when you disappeared after that first night we spent together, I was convinced I'd imagined you, because I couldn't see how you'd escaped."

"I had three thousand years to develop techniques to escape places. None of them ever worked."

The sadness in the words tugged at her, and she wrapped her arms around him. "You're not in there anymore. You're here. With me."

"What if I'm imprisoned again?"

You won't be alone. She almost said it. Almost made a promise that would be terrifying to keep. Could she make that kind of commitment?

She leaned up and kissed him, giving him a different kind of vow. "Never. You're free, Azrael. And I'm going to make sure it stays that way."

"Your optimism might be misplaced."

"Worrywart. Let's go find some of your many-times-removed cousins."

"I am not related to silvers," he grumbled.

"You're right, they're much nicer. First things first. Clothes." Most of which were strewn on the floor. Whoever searched her apartment hadn't cared about the mess they'd made. While she managed to gather what she needed, she put her brain to work. How to find dragons?

Once she'd managed to put an outfit together, she also packed a suitcase with extras. She pointed to it. "Send that to your cave for the next time I visit, would you?"

He opened his mouth as if to say something then smiled. The suitcase disappeared. As did her bed.

She frowned at him but couldn't be mad, not when he winked and said, "We'll need that later."

At least he planned on a later. The thought teased, but she couldn't allow herself to be distracted.

"Now to find you some dragons. I am pretty sure I heard Babette use the last name Silvergrace. Let me see if the cops left my laptop." They hadn't. They'd also taken her tablet, and she'd long ago lost her phone.

"Dammit!" She stomped her foot. "They took everything."

"Do we need to retrieve your belongings?"

She blinked at him. "Raid the cops for my stuff? Yeah. No. Probably not a good idea. We can use just the library. They have computers and internet access."

She grabbed his hand as they left her place, using the excuse they shouldn't lose track of each other. He appeared amused by the idea and yet held her hand. Said not much as she took him underground into a subway. Although he did tense a bit when the train arrived and again as it left.

"It's safe," she murmured, leaning into him.

"Obviously or it wouldn't have so many people aboard. Do you realize the speed of its travel makes it dangerous?"

"Very. But it's fast and will drop us a block from the library. Come on."

He might not like the subway, but he understood to hold his ground. He didn't let anyone push him around and, by extension, offered her the same protection. She didn't have to jostle with anyone for position on the escalator.

They emerged at street level, and she led him to the library where he stood out in his cape and leather pants. Yet, no one said a thing. The past decade had done much to immune people to the sight of those who enjoyed dressing for cosplay.

The computers were all in use, meaning they had to wait. He didn't like waiting.

"Why can we not simply remove that person?"

he asked as an older gentleman browsed some interesting ads on a certain shopping network.

"Because taking someone's turn will get us tossed out of the library. Just be patient."

"I don't want to be patient," he grumbled.

She dragged him between the stacks of books, moving farther back to a dusty corner of encyclopedias that rarely saw foot traffic.

She shoved him against a shelf and leaned into him. "Calm down. We'll find the other dragons and convince them to help us."

"I don't see how that will help. They have no mages."

"But they have resources obviously." She couldn't help but remember how easily they'd located her in the mental institution and arranged to have her removed.

"What if they won't provide aid?"

She shrugged. "Then we go to plan B."

"We have a second plan?"

"Not yet, but I'm sure we'll figure something out if it gets that far."

His hands looped around her waist and drew her close. "It is a good thing you're helping me."

"Oh, why is that?"

"Because you make waiting a lot more palatable." His mouth touched hers with a kiss that ignited her desire.

Never mind they'd had sex not that long ago. He embraced her, and all her senses came alive.

She wore yoga pants that were easily pushed down. His hand fitted between her thighs and found her wet. He turned her and had her gripping the bookcase as he slid in from behind. She caught a moan by biting her lower lip.

The pleasure filled her just as he stretched her, his breath hot on her ear as he toyed with the lobe. The hard heat of him thrusting. One hand reaching between her legs to play with her clit. The other cupping a breast.

She came just as hard as every other time, squeezing him. Gasping. Shaking and melting happily into his arms when he turned her around and enfolded her in a hug.

She could have stayed there forever. And who knows, she might have if the screaming hadn't started.

Chapter Fifteen

Using predictive text type, Going stir-crazy, in need of...

"How much longer do we have to wait?" Babette whined. She knew she'd reached the height of annoying when Luc abruptly left the room.

Elspeth, being her best friend, couldn't follow. "Soon."

"You've been saying that for like two days." Two long days of scouring social media for possible horsemen sightings. Two days of the aunts and everyone with access to old history books poring through them looking for answers.

Two days of being cooped up and getting tapping feet. The urge to act.

"If you're feeling restless, then go for a walk," Elspeth suggested.

"Have you looked out the window? It's raining."

"You don't say." Elspeth craned from her spot on the couch to peek out the window.

Babette rolled her eyes. "Sometimes I have to wonder if you're fucking with me or not. You can predict the future and yet are just as bad as the weather network."

"All weather has a positive. Even rain. If you want to stay dry, bring an umbrella. I might also suggest some lip gloss."

What an odd suggestion. "I don't do makeup unless I'm clubbing or looking to get some. Since we're on high alert, I don't see either happening any time soon."

"Put on the war paint or don't, that changes nothing. But you really need to go for a walk."

"You're being awfully insistent. Why?" Babette asked, unable to hide her innate suspicion. "Have you seen something? Do I need to bring a weapon?" Being a dragon was awesome in most cases, but things that went boom truly did bring a little thrill as well.

"Nothing in the garden will hurt you. But if you stick around, you might be scarred for life, because I am about to have very loud sex with my mate. So unless you'd like to watch and listen…"

"Ew. Gross." She covered her eyes. "I am out of here."

Babette stalked from the suite in the Silvergrace manor Elspeth had taken over while she and Luc visited. Usually they stayed in Luc's castle—which he'd technically stolen from its previous owner, but the village didn't seem to mind. Apparently, Luc was a much better lord of the manor than the previous guy.

It wasn't raining hard outside, just a slight drizzle, so she eschewed the umbrella. She brought a gun, however, tucked into the back of her pants, hidden under her jean jacket. The fine droplets were enough to dew her skin and make a mockery of any semblance of control over her hair.

As if she cared how she looked. She wasn't trying to impress anyone. As a matter of fact, she was kind of done with people at the moment. It seemed she'd barely had a moment to herself since shit hit the fan a few months ago.

To think she used lament the fact the Septs had to hide their existence, and yet it turned out being revealed was the most stressful thing of all. Not only did she have to watch herself even more than before, it meant her routines were interrupted and her space crowded as visitors filled the mansion to the brim. And they didn't leave, because, of late, it seemed they dealt with nothing but emergencies.

They also had a preponderance of people

falling in love. Even Elspeth, who'd always been considered off, had found herself a mate.

"Always a bridesmaid, never a bride," Babette grumbled as she trudged through the garden. It was actually quite lovely when wet. Leaves glistened, and the greenery smelled more potent than usual.

The sun was hidden behind thick gray clouds, leaving a somber cast all around. A faint fog hung, restricting her vision. The shifting lines of the mist kept drawing her attention. Nothing there. Nothing there.

Someone in a robe.

Wait. What?

She veered her gaze sharply back to the left and saw a figure standing still, a cloak stretched head to toe, framing a tall yet slender shape. At their back, a pale horse.

Which apparently was a cross between bile green and toasted marshmallow.

It matched its rider.

Holy shit, one of the horsemen was in the garden.

Hands encased in pale gloves rose to pull back a hood, revealing a face that was delicate in nature, gentle even, with big eyes, the pupils dark, the cheeks flushed pink, the lips full and red, the skin parchment fine. The figure's beauty was offset by the wildness of the hair, a writhing mass of tendrils that thickened and thinned, moving all the time, as if the person floated underwater.

"Are you here to attack?" she asked as the rider made no move.

"I haven't decided yet." The voice had a feminine lilt to it.

"What are you waiting for?" Babette appeared relaxed, and yet she was ready to move if needed.

"A reason. Thus far you've not given me one."

"Would you like me to rectify that?" she said with a huge dose of sarcasm.

The lips curved. "I see humor still lives in this time."

"Life would suck without laughter. I don't suppose we can take this conversation inside. It's kind of wet out here."

"It's nice to feel the rain again." The rider lifted her face to the droplets, eyes closed, lips parted as if to taste the droplets.

"You live somewhere arid?" A dumb thing to ask. She'd seen the video of the riders of the apocalypse rising from a hole in the desert.

"I was a prisoner for a long time in a place with no sun, no moon, no stars. And definitely no weather. You have no idea how lucky you are."

On an impulse, Babette asked, "What's your name?"

It took a moment before she replied. "I am Jeebrelle."

"Babette, but most people call me Babs."

"Are you the messenger for your king?" asked Jeebrelle.

"I guess." Babette shrugged. "I do what I'm told to. Sometimes it involves passing along messages. Other times getting rid of threats." She casually tossed that out there to see the effect.

Jeebrelle cocked her head and smiled again. A small coy thing. "You are interesting, Babette the Silver."

Having met Azrael and seen his giant dragon, she didn't feel stupid at all asking, "What color are you?"

"Can't you tell?" Curiosity laced the query.

"You're a mixture of scents, none of them dragon," she admitted.

Jeebrelle's eyes widened. "How can you not know the scent of a dragon mage?"

"Because your asses were banned," was her retort. "On account a bunch of the mages used their magic for evil. Were you one of them?" She went on the offense.

Jeebrelle looked more pensive than worried. "You banned all magic wielders?"

"Not me, personally. My ancestors did, according to what we've been able to glean."

"I would call you a liar, but I guess it is possible. Our kind was never very populous. Even the strictest breeding didn't always result in success."

Jeebrelle tapped her lower lip. "How many magic users exist now?"

"None," Babette stated. Only to correct herself. "Possibly one. The king's brother seems to have some kind of ability."

"One?" Jeebrelle blinked. "That is unexpected and disappointing."

"Care to explain why?"

"No. Because that would lead to even more questions and more time wasted talking when I need to be working."

"Working on what?"

"Sowing seeds. Starting the change needed."

"Wait a second. What's that supposed to mean?" Babette asked.

"It means I have a lot of work to accomplish and little time. It was an unexpected pleasure speaking with you, Babette the Silver. Perhaps we'll meet again." Jeebrelle winked before whirling, the cloak rising in a swirl of fabric that disintegrated as if absorbed by the mist. When it cleared, the rider and her horse were gone.

Babette stood staring. Mostly because she really hoped Jeebrelle came back. Which made her all kinds of stupid.

Hadn't she learned her lesson the last time she got involved with a bad girl?

Apparently not, because she went back to the house to do a little more research. Not much as it turned out because, by the time she'd made herself a giant snack and settled in front of a computer to search, the whole mansion went on alert.

She raced to the command center—which held a pool table that flipped into a holographic deck—standing along with others, eyeing a live stream on *Facebook*. The picture jostled and had a lot of heavy breathing and screaming.

"Is that a swarm of locusts?" she asked, squinting at the flying specks.

"It is happening right now at the library."

"Our library? Why are we still here?" Babette raced from the house and in moments had taken to the air. It would take her a few minutes in dragon shape to reach the area of the densest bug infestation.

The thing she'd seen in that jerky footage.

The figure made partially of smoke.

Was the enemy finally making its move?

Chapter Sixteen

The seventh vow: Forget the first vow. Nothing wrong with certain distractions.

"What's happening?" Daphne righted her clothes quickly as the screams escalated.

"Something bad." Which seemed obvious to him given the level of audible panic. "Wait here while I investigate."

"Like hell. I want to know what's happening, too."

"Stay close to me." He edged out from between the stacks of books, and the hum of panic—and excitement— immediately hit. Some people were gesticulating wildly, their faces ripe with terror. Others pressed against the few windows, apparently intrigued by what they could see outside.

Rather than join them, Daphne slid into the

vacated seat of the computer. "Let me do a quick search and see if I can find an address for the Silvergraces."

"While you are seeking, I shall endeavor to pinpoint the dilemma causing the chaos." Given he saw somebody plucking a large insect from their hair, he thought it actually a good idea she remained indoors in relative safety.

He, on the other hand, headed straight into the danger. He strode for the doors, where a group of humans huddled, panicked and exclaiming. The snippets he caught only cemented his decision.

"...just appeared out of nowhere. A cloud of them. Buzzing and attacking."

"Are they bees?" was a fearful query.

"No. Bigger and uglier. More beetle like."

The locusts had arrived. It could mean only one thing. The Shaitan had begun sowing the seeds of destruction.

Azrael slammed through the library door and emerged into a storm of chaos. So much to take in. Flying insects zipped through the air, the hum of thousands of wings drowning all other sounds. There were people outside who either raced about in a panic, screaming and flailing, or aiming their little talking boxes to take pictures while swatting at the locusts swarming to attack. How long before they regretted that decision? Had they not been taught to protect themselves from the flesh eaters?

He almost winced as the first human realized his grave error. Luckily, his truly strident screams as he died painfully sent the others running. If they didn't run, then too bad for them. He didn't have time to waste.

While the humans should take cover from the flesh-eating menace, none dared to touch Azrael. He wore a shield of magic that repulsed them, kept them from touching his body.

The swarm didn't appear out of nowhere. Not in a city. He'd seen this kind of thing before. In the past. It was usually a Shaitan behind it.

He glanced past the dense net of insects, seeking the center. Someone guided the locusts. There was magic pushing them to attack. Not to mention they must have been snared from somewhere and transported here. That kind of concentrated effort took a lot of magic and would exhaust the person casting.

Break the focus of the caster and the recoil would handle the rest. He just needed to find the Shaitan. He fingered the item in his pocket, a thing he'd carved during his prison time. It used to be in the alcove of his cave.

It might come in handy now. As would the Dracinore dagger by his side.

Could it affect the Shaitan? There had to be something better than stuffing them into bottles and other containers.

Only one way to find out if the knife would work. He needed to get close enough to wield it.

Putting his fingers to his lips, he blew a bone whistle that he kept fitted on his finger. It gave a sharp, strident note with a zap of power. The bone was all that remained of his loyal steed. Cursed at the same moment as Azrael—it was one of the few that survived the plunge underground. They were partners for a thousand years before his steed finally met its doom. Azrael killed the giant worm too late to save his horse. The meat made a fine stew, and he kept the bones, carving them, making them into figurines. Jewelry. But it was the ring that he imbued with the symbols that provided the connection to the soul of his lost stallion. When his magic returned, he was pleased to see that all he needed was to blow into the bone whistle to summon his old friend.

From nowhere, literally, his white horse arrived, no longer a suit of bones, the sign of a starving soul. It had been feeding well on magic since their release. His stallion's coat gleamed and shone distinctly against the dark swarm as it galloped. It neighed as it cantered to a stop and tossed its head.

"My friend." He greeted his steed with a soft hand. "Shall we ride?"

It stamped its feet in agreement. With permission granted, he swung onto Lemagrag's back, not needing a saddle or reins. A good mount kept its rider seated, and a good rider knew how to hold on. In this case, he kept his seat with only his legs, as he needed his hands to cast spells. No need to guide. Lemagrag understood better than most what he had to do. This wasn't their first, or even hundredth, fight.

He leaned into the flowing mane, feeling it tickle his skin, and whispered, "Bring me close to the Shaitan."

"Neigh."

At a rapid gallop, his steed speared through the cloud of bugs. The locusts tumbled and crashed in their hurry to move out of the way. They didn't want to touch the horse or Azrael. That was both good and bad, because it made it easy to spot the disturbance they caused, making an easy target of them.

"Up ahead," he said, knowing Lema had already spotted their target.

The Shaitan hovered about twenty feet above ground, ignoring Azrael, thinking to pretend he was harmless.

Its delusion amused. Three thousand years and they still had to play games.

Azrael thrust out a hand and wound some magic around his fingers. He then whispered into it, a soft word, before tossing it up into the smoky bottom half of the Shaitan.

The ball of power exploded, which his enemy

expected, and ignored. What the Shaitan couldn't avoid was the funnel that was created by the explosion. The churning air tried to catch the smoke and shred its cohesion.

The Shaitan tugged free with a screech, but it didn't flee. It swooped, aiming for Azrael, its face drawn and cavernous. The mouth opened wide enough to swallow him whole, from the waist down, pure smoke.

Azrael pulled the dagger made of Dracinore, the most dangerous metal he knew. Even holding it with a glove, the exposed blade affected his dragon side. He felt weak.

Human.

Fragile.

It might have frightened him if he'd not spent three thousand years without magic. He'd had all that time to learn how to fight—and win.

The Shaitan dove at Azrael, and he ducked, his blade slashing, having no effect on the smoke. He needed to test with a more direct hit. Perhaps if he struck the Shaitan when it was solid.

Slipping from his horse—who reacted to the exposed blade by turning to skin and bones—he dropped into a half-crouch and waited for the Shaitan to return.

The thing, part ghost, part monster, paced the air above. A wailing wraith that laughed and babbled, "It feels so good. Their fear. Their anxiety. So delicious."

"You're a parasite," Azrael declared, trying to draw its attention.

"And?" The Shaitan bobbed midair. Smiled too wide for its head.

"You don't belong in this world."

"But we like it."

"The humans won't stand for you attacking them."

"As if they have a choice." It drifted lower. "They are but dumb animals. Barely paying attention. Arguing all the time. By the time they realize what's happening, it will be over. The world will belong to us, and the Iblis shall return."

"The Iblis will destroy Earth if released, and then where will you be?"

"Moving on to the next plane. And the next. We are not called the destroyer for nothing."

"Seems like a pretty lofty name for a guy who has to stay inside during windstorms."

The insult actually managed to punch its expression.

"We are invulnerable. Can you say the same? What if you had your parts scattered?"

"I'd be dead."

"We wouldn't be, though. We always find each other."

"Do you? What if you were chopped up really small?"

It stiffened, becoming corporeal for a moment. Angry. "There is nothing that can do that."

"Are you sure?" He smiled. "Rumor has it there is a way to kill you." He watched for a reaction.

It was mirth. "Then you are misinformed. Nothing in this plane has the power to harm us."

"What if it came from somewhere else?" he said, and while the Shaitan was distracted, he dove and swung the dagger, aiming for the Shaitan's midsection, only it dissolved and dispersed before he could even touch it.

"Do you really think your mud weapons can harm us?"

He wasn't about to admit he'd really hoped the dagger would slit the Shaitan in two, but he'd come prepared in case it didn't. He pulled the carved flask from his pocket. The lid popped off with a press of his thumb, and the hole to the inside gaped.

This managed to scare the Shaitan. It turned almost translucent. "I will not be trapped again."

"You should have thought of that before sending a storm of locusts."

Rather than reply, the Shaitan went to flee, which was when Azrael aimed the true magic he'd been holding on to, a much larger magical vortex that didn't need to be touching the smoke to tug at it. The wind funnel sucked at the Shaitan as Azrael positioned the flask at the tapered end. Once the tornado drew in the Shaitan, he would funnel its essence into the container. Inscribed with intricate spells, it would form a new prison.

"No. No. No!" It strained against the pull and began drawing away, ripping its smoky tail free over and over, meaning he only had useless wisps. He poured more of his magic into it. Began winning the tug of war with the Shaitan. It was being sucked into the vortex. Soon he'd have it locked away.

"No. Let go of me!"

The sharp scream and protest drew his attention.

Daphne.

The distraction proved enough for the Shaitan to escape and the vortex to collapse. The monster fled, and Azrael whirled to see Daphne on the front steps of the library, struggling in a second pair of smoky arms.

There were two of them here.

A trap!

The Shaitan from the museum, with his slick dark hair, and cinnamon scent with a hint of cardamom, held Daphne in its grip. But she wasn't going easily. "Let me go." She even tried blowing hot wet huffs of air, as if the Shaitan were a candle.

"Unhand her!" Azrael boomed as he moved in their direction. A sharp whistle brought Lema hurtling, hooves sparking when they struck. His steed had obviously been feeding on the magic it needed to take and hold a shape. It galloped past Azrael, heading for Daphne and the Shaitan.

Would Lema make it in time?

Just in case, Azrael drew back the arm holding the dagger. At maximum impact, he rolled it forward and released the dagger. It went spinning, hilt over tip.

Perhaps the Dracinore metal did pose a danger, because the Shaitan released Daphne and launched itself out of the path of the dagger. Interesting. But he had no time to test it further because the dagger went clattering just as Lema reached the Shaitan and reared, a massive beast on two legs about to stomp.

The horse went through the smoke, separating it, which would weaken the Shaitan. The more magic it had to use, the more it tired. It would need to replenish shortly. He just needed to hold it off a little bit longer. Azrael ran for the Shaitan, stave in hand. He spun it, disrupting the smoky nature of the Shaitan, forcing it into a physical shape that he could hit.

How much pain did the Shaitan feel when his rod ripped through the smoke? It must not enjoy it because it did try to dodge, but it didn't grimace. Didn't make a sound at all as it dodged and threw attacks.

It wouldn't be long before it ran out of juice.

Separate, the Shaitan could be repelled. But put them together...He'd rather not deal with that particular situation.

To his surprise, a human male ran out of a nearby building. Rather than flee, the fellow with the portly mid-section, uncombed hair, and thick-rimmed glasses ran with determination toward Azrael. The human held a strange contraption with a handle that ended in a rectangular hole. The whole thing buzzed, and even the Shaitan paused to see what would happen when the man got close enough.

When the object began sucking smoke, Azrael might have lost his jaw on the ground for a moment. A portable whirlpool of air that siphoned. Would the wonders of this time never cease?

Perhaps they could beat the threat of the Shaitan.

Apparently, the monster realized it too. For a moment its face appeared, the eyes staring in disbelief at the innocuous thing sucking at his midsection.

Then it glared. Hotly.

The human yelped and jumped away, but Azrael noticed the weakness of the attack. The Shaitan was running out of power.

Before he could use that to his advantage, the monster bolted straight into the air, a dark streak that entered an even blacker rift. It closed too quickly to follow. It had escaped, and since he'd not seen where it landed, he couldn't follow.

The good thing, it wouldn't return for a while until it recharged. Now to deal with the other one. He turned to see if the other menace would stand against him or flee. Apparently it had a third choice in mind, as the Shaitan dragged Daphne through another gate.

Her panicked gaze was the last thing he saw.

Chapter Seventeen

Fuck all the previous vows. Only one thing mattered. His mate.

T he Shaitan had taken Daphne.

The shock dropped Azrael to his knees, his mind blown. He didn't understand why.

Why did her capture and probable death bother him? Why her and not the countless others he'd seen taken? He'd seen so much death. Many of those deaths people, or a beloved companion like Lema, close to him. It had hurt. But he'd accepted it. And once even had to deal the killing blow.

But Daphne getting kidnapped by his worst enemy?

Forget nonchalance. He couldn't just pretend he didn't care.

He seethed with emotion. Raged at the temerity

of the monster. Daphne was no match for the Shaitan.

Which led to terror, actual blood-numbing fear, as he realized the kind of torture she might endure. He had to find her, but he had no idea where they'd gone. The magical tracker he'd activated earlier remained silent. It didn't emit a single pulse. Either she was hidden by magic, or…

No. He wouldn't even think it.

He had to concentrate on finding her. But how?

The sudden arrival of a silver dragon didn't improve his mood as the female he'd met before came to stand by his side.

"What do you want?" he snarled, fingers flexing by his side. Killing something might help with his tension.

"Is that any way to greet an ally?"

Azrael whirled to glare at her. "What makes you think we are allies?"

"Because I'd say we have a common goal. Getting rid of those evil genie fellows."

"And how do you propose we do that? You've already admitted there are no mages. How else are we supposed to trap them?"

"There's got to be some other way." The woman—Babette, if he recalled correctly—eyed the human who'd so bravely and foolishly engaged the enemy. "What was the nerdy basement dweller doing before I got here?" she asked, pointing to the human.

"He tried to give aid brandishing a device with suction."

Her eyes widened. "He tried to vacuum a genie." She tapped her chin. "It's actually kind of brilliant." She eyed him. "Was it working?"

"To the extent it could. The inhalation wasn't strong enough to truly trap the Shaitan."

"But we can vacuum them? That's actually kind of cool. And gives me an idea. We need a bigger, stronger vacuum. Say like a Dyson or something."

"Even if you could inhale them, how will you keep the Shaitan contained?"

"Stick it in a jar and cork it. Isn't that what you guys did before?" She wrinkled her nose.

"It's not that simple. Protection must be placed on the vessel. Spells to keep the Shaitan from simply shattering the container."

Sirens blared in the distance, getting nearer. The silver, who wore only a flimsy dress and no shoes, glanced to her left. "We should get out of here before the cops arrive. At least the aunts will have dealt with the video footage. Hopefully nothing goes viral with your face in it. That first one of you and your buddies emerging from that sink-hole in the desert was a social media nightmare. I think you out-trended the white cat."

He grimaced. He had no idea about half of

what she'd said, so he stuck to the simple part. "Goodbye."

"Oh no, dude. You can't leave yet. You know what that thing is, how to fight it. Plus, you're one of us."

There was probably disdain in his gaze. "Hardly like you. And I do not have time to argue. I must locate Daphne."

"Can't you snap your fingers and teleport us to where she is?"

"No," he said flatly. Unlike the Shaitan, his magic had more restrictions.

"But I've seen you teleport."

The word wasn't one he comprehended, but he did grasp her intent. "I can only open passages to places I've seen." That was the simple way of putting it. It was actually more than just having been somewhere. He needed to recall the precise imprint of a place to be able to rip a path between his location and the one he sought.

"What if I showed you a picture?"

"Does it have smell? Can you make me breathe its air?"

"No. Pity. That would have made it faster and gotten us out of this rain," she grumbled, glaring at the droplets as they fell.

The deluge did not stop the humans from emerging from their hiding places to examine the locusts left behind. To once more take videos with their technology.

He tuned in to her last words.

"…the house isn't far."

"I am going nowhere with you," he stated brusquely. As if he'd ally with a silver.

"Do you want to find Daphne?"

"Was I not already clear on that?"

"So you know where she is? How to get there fastest? Because if you can't teleport, then that means you're flying, which takes time. Plus, we actually know where at least one of those genies has made their lair."

His interest was piqued. "You will relate the location."

"In time, dude. First, we need to make a viable plan. But in order to make sure it will work, we need you. Need every bit of knowledge you have about those genies so we can wipe them out, once and for all."

He almost scoffed at her bold claim, but three thousand years had done much to soothe his arrogance. This era had tools and knowledge he'd never imagined. Perhaps there was an easier way than giving up his life.

"If you must insist, lead me to your city." He whistled for Lema. His stallion arrived and pranced in place by his side.

"Dude… What kind of horse is that?"

"A special one."

"And what color would you say it is?"

"Why does it matter?" he asked tersely.

"Just curious. I don't suppose your friends have a red one?"

"Yes." He snapped.

"Just one more question. Is your horse dead? Does it eat brains?"

"It's not alive in the usual sense. And it doesn't eat flesh." Lema fed on the natural magical energy flowing through this world, without it, his steed returned to being a soul trapped inside a piece of bone. He swung up onto Lema. "If you're done, lead the way and I shall follow your chariot."

Babette huffed. "I had to come quick, so I flew. Only barely remembered to bring something to wear."

Meaning she needed a ride. He sighed as he held out a hand. "He can take us both."

"Before I get on that thing, please tell me your horse has a name."

"Lemagrag."

She blinked at him. "You're kidding, right?"

"I fail to see the humor."

"Anyone who's watched the Smurfs will get it," she muttered. "Tell me, do you know of little blue people who live in toadstools?"

"The *frumm* aren't all blue, and they haven't

lived in mushrooms in a thousand years at least. Once we tamed them, they learned quickly."

Babette eschewed his hand and vaulted onto the wide back of his stallion. "Hi ho, Silver, and away," she muttered as she held on to him.

As Lema leaped into motion, Babette squeaked, "Could we at least be a little more discreet? Auntie is going to kill me because there's no way someone isn't posting a video of this."

"You seek to be hidden from the humans?" He pushed some magic and said, "Done."

Babette just had to question. "How? Are we invisible?"

"Essentially. The raindrops have been turned into mirrors reflecting away from us, creating an illusion."

"Handy. Can you teach me how to do it?"

"No."

"Why not?"

"You're not a mage."

"Is this some sexist thing?" Babette huffed.

"Hardly. Some of the finest magic users I've known were female."

"Could you bottle it?"

"No."

He was sure Babette would have kept asking him stupid questions if Lema had not launched himself into the air, shadowy wings extending from his sides. He kept their shield of invisibility despite their ascent into the sky.

"Which way?" he asked.

Babette, over her initial shock, gave him directions. And then more questions. Upon more questions.

If he weren't worried about Daphne, he would have tossed her off. Thankfully it wasn't long until they arrived at a well-kept palace made of stone. Not the largest he'd seen. Not even close to what he remembered his kind preferring during his tenure on Earth.

Perhaps the silver was one of the poor cousins. In that case, how much could she actually help?

As Lema landed, his hooves struck and dented a metal chariot before alighting in front of some steps. Babette flung herself off the stallion first, and he soon followed, patting his steed on his nose. Dismissing him.

With a neigh, Lema galloped off as a commotion arose. People, most of them dragons, poured from all the openings: a double door at the top of the steps, a few windows, the balconies. Two dragons even alit on the rooftop.

Babette walked toward them, hands raised. "Don't shoot or eat him. He's with me."

She thought to protect him? It was almost amusing.

"You brought a man home?" someone hollered.

"Don't be so jealous, Veronica. Not my fault I'm popular even with the boys."

He took offense at the silver claiming him as a bedmate. "I am taken. By a human. I'm here because she said you had information."

"And you expect us to just hand over that info?" asked an older woman, also a silver, standing on the step.

Babette was the one to explain. "Remember those smoky dude sightings? He knows how to fight them."

"Sightings?" He zoned in on the plural of the word. "The Shaitan have been spotted? Where? Doing what?"

"We should discuss this inside. In privacy," said the older female.

"That's no fun," someone muttered. But the silvers obeyed, most of them disappearing from whence they appeared until only Babette and the older woman remained.

She angled her head. "Shall we?"

"Who are you?" he asked.

The woman, with regal bearing and a short silver hairstyle, offered a faint smile. "I am Zahra Silvergrace, and you are?"

"Azrael."

"What's your family name?"

His lip curled. "Mages don't need one, as we are unique."

"Surely you weren't the only guy with the name Azrael."

"I was the only dragon mage bearing it," he stated.

"So you admit to being a mage?"

"Why would I hide it?" he queried, only to smirk. "Or is this about the fact you banished them? Perhaps I should mention I will not voluntarily exile myself for the sins of others. And I wouldn't recommend forcing the issue."

"I would never dream of it. But I am curious. We didn't even know mages existed until recently," Zahra stated as they stepped inside the house.

It was nicer within than expected. The walls were smooth and painted a light gray, the floors nicely fitted stone.

"Because we were wiped from the histories, obviously." His lip curled.

"Not all of them. We did manage to find an old story. It spoke of thirteen who bound themselves to the evil ones, vowing to return if they ever escaped." Zahra pursed her lips and paused outside a closed door. "It was thought to be a legend. A story much like the fairy tales the humans enjoy."

"Forgotten and then banished." He huffed through his nose. "I am beginning to regret my decision. This world is not the one I sacrificed for."

"What's wrong with it?" Babette asked, cocking her head.

"For one, it is overrun with humans." Who weren't all that bad. At least Daphne wasn't. He reserved the right to eat the ones that irritated him.

"And two?"

"Isn't one enough?" he exclaimed. "They've covered the world like a spreading disease. What used to be vast swatches of untouched land are now dotted with buildings and roads. Electrical lines are changing the magical lei of the planet. Nothing is as I remember." He'd emerged into an alien world, and the only time he didn't feel overwhelmed and afraid? When he was with Daphne.

"You're talking like you've been alive hundreds of years."

"Try thousands. Bound by a spell and locked away until I was needed."

"Wait, you've been in prison?" Babette exclaimed. "And you say Silvers are bad?"

He scowled. "It was a prison of my own choosing. We were told the world would have need of us and so chose to be bound."

Zahra reached out and laid a hand on his. Soft. As was her gaze as she said, "I can't begin to imagine what it must have been like to sacrifice so much. And for so long. The culture shock when you emerged must have been awful."

Her understanding was welcome and annoying all at once. "I don't need your pity."

"And I would never think to demean your sacrifice with that kind of emotion. But I will say you are not alone in this fight. You have allies. People who can help."

"I don't need anyone's help."

"Do you or don't you want to find your girl-friend and beat that genie?" Babette snapped. "Or are you actually here to bring about the apocalypse?"

"What?" He frowned at her. "What are talking about?"

"As if you don't know. There's all kinds of stories about the four horsemen who appear when the end of world is nigh," Babette exclaimed. "They'll bring plagues and famine and death and war and all kinds of things no one really wants."

"All true. If the Shaitan are not dealt with, then your world is doomed. Despite what you believe, I am not here to start the apocalypse but to stop it."

Chapter Eighteen

Missing her pink unicorn onesie.

"The End" by the Doors, crooned by Jim Morrison, played over and over. And over. It emerged from the connected speakers in the condominium her kidnappers brought her to.

It was annoying more than scary. Did her captors not know how to play anything else? Perhaps she should introduce them to some different artists.

Or maybe, Daphne decided, she'd do nothing at all. She'd reached her terror quotient for the day.

It began with her freezing because Mr. Smoky decided to kidnap her. Then it turned into frustration when she flailed and screamed to no avail. A coldest fear did start to sink in when the genie opened some kind of inter-dimensional hole, but she handled it without peeing herself. Thank you, SyFy Channel, for making her a little prepared for the freakiness of travelling through one. She'd clenched tight as she was yanked through a rip in the very air.

The two times before, Azrael had put her to sleep to protect her from it. This time, she was thrust into it wide-awake. Aware.

She emerged into the vastest nothing she could have imagined. No, she would have never imagined this kind of emptiness. She wasn't even a speck in this place. She was less than nothing. A—

What was that? Did the darkness seem just a touch blacker over there? Was it moving, coming for her? Reaching?

The emergence into reality proved jarring. She fell to her knees on carpeted flooring, her fingers digging into the plush cream pile. She only realized she hadn't been breathing when she choked in a breath, then another, expelling frost from her lungs, taking in real air. Her stomach had been left behind at the library, and her head spun.

That was an experience she didn't want to repeat.

Someone jabbered in a language she didn't understand, but the reply was in English. "Speak the language so she understands."

"Barbaric noise." The disdain proved thick. "Why did we capture a human?"

"Not just any human. *His* human," said Mr. Smoky.

Mr. Friend had a more nasally tenor. "Servant?"

"Concubine."

"Disgusting flesh lovers." Huffed with a moue of displeasure.

Rude. And she almost exclaimed it, only to bite her lip at the last second. She thought about standing. Her head wasn't spinning round and round anymore. However, just as she thought about giving the vertical a try, something sniffed her.

What. The. Hell.

A gagging noise followed. "She reeks of him." Which apparently was gross.

"We know. Recall how attached they are to their mates. Which is why he will bargain for her." A hand gripped her hair and yanked her head back. "With your life being held in the balance, he is sure to trade."

Daphne didn't share that certainty.

"And if he doesn't?" Mr. Friend asked.

The cold words matched the expression on Mr. Smoky's face. "Then she dies."

Having properly scared her, they flipped to their other language, meaning she was left huddled on the floor, feeling pretty freaking screwed. She knew Azrael wouldn't trade any of the magic seals for her life. The man had endured a three-thousand-year prison to fight the bad guys. He wasn't about to ruin that sacrifice for her.

Only a man who loved her might be that foolish.

A noble hero like Azrael would do what was right and let her die.

She hoped to at least have a good last meal. She certainly had some recent and epic memories. They were the only things that kept her from completely snapping when she was dragged to a bedroom. She feared the worst. The kind of fear only a woman in the control of a sadistic man understood.

But they didn't touch her in that way. They locked the door when they left. The music started playing not long after, and she paced her comfortable prison cell.

They appeared to be in a condominium. Top floor with a view over a city. Not her city, she might add. She didn't recognize any of the tall buildings but noted the tropical trees dotting the sidewalks. Florida maybe? Or the opposite coast, in California?

The room they'd placed her in was a bedroom, obviously in use, with a walk-in closet full of a teen's clothes, piles of it on the floor, and a hidden stash of weed in a shoebox. She tucked the joint away for later. The room obviously belonged to someone. What happened to them?

She hugged herself as she sat on the window

ledge. It was only about three inches wide, and the window was the kind that didn't open. She stared outside, wondering what would happen to her.

If only she'd remained in the library. But when someone yelled about the guy on the white horse riding into the bug storm, she'd known it was Azrael and had to...watch? Because it wasn't as if she could make a difference.

She emerged into a nightmare, locusts everywhere, and she slapped at them when they tried to land. Only when the swarm died down did she see Azrael and realize he didn't need any help.

She'd watched in amazement as he showed his skill as a fighter. He ran into battle without hesitation, wielding his staff just like he had in the museum, but this time, she knew it was real.

He fought with skill, hitting the genie, having no effect on the smoke. Until that guy emerged with his portable vacuum and went after the smoke, pulling a Ghostbuster on it.

Ultimately, it failed, but the idea was intriguing. She wondered if Azrael would think to buy a bigger vacuum with a canister that was genie proof. Even if he did, it wouldn't be in time to save her.

The last thing she'd heard before getting locked away was Mr. Smoky saying, "The ransom request was sent."

The countdown to her death was on. She couldn't even blame Azrael. For one, he didn't even know where she was. Two, the fate of the world shouldn't be put in jeopardy for her. Three, why would he risk himself for her?

Why did this have to happen now? They'd been so good together. Azrael knew how to make her body sing. Perhaps, eventually, he would have loved her.

If only she could have had more time.

She pressed her fingers to the glass as she stared sightlessly outside and breathed, "Oh Azrael, I wish you were here with me." Her forehead twinged. A whoosh of something slammed through her, hard enough she fell on the floor.

She was still face down when she heard Azrael say, "How did I get here?"

Chapter Nineteen

When someone calls you crazy, thank them as you hand over your beer because it's time to retain that title.

"Where did he go?"

The dragons blinked in astonishment as the mage who'd been involved in a group discussion in their boardroom popped out of sight.

"That's rude," exclaimed Babette. "I was talking to him."

"More like he was about to mansplain how he was going to save all the poor little dragon girls from the big bad genie. Ha." Aimi snorted. "Probably left before we could beat the hell out of him."

"Please, we all know where he's gone and what he's going to do." At a few blank looks, Adrienne huffed. "He's going to find his human girlfriend to, you know." She made a gesture with her two hands along with a squeaking noise in case it wasn't clear.

"Now?" queried Aimi. "Seems like a bad time to be thinking about sex."

"Tell that to the guy in love," Babette sassed back.

Adrienne was the one to orate the dubiousness of her claim. "He's a horseman of the apocalypse. He's not going to be distracted by a human."

Babette shrugged. "He likes her. A lot."

"He can't like her that much already. Didn't they just meet?" Adrienne questioned.

"The guy was locked up for three thousand years. I'm surprised he got out of bed yet," muttered someone else in the room.

"What's really surprising is how after all that time alone, one of his arms isn't oversized from jerking off." Babette noticed these kinds of things.

"He probably kept switching hands. It's a thing apparently," Adrienne confided.

"I'll help him forget all about her," Veronica, one of the lesser cousins, with punk rock hair, offered.

"Don't be such a slut. A man his age needs someone with maturity." Aunt Yolanda fluffed her hair.

"What if he didn't leave but was kidnapped?" Babette proffered, only to be met with scorn. Yet she'd been closest to Azrael when the air ripped. No other word for it. The very essence of the world split, and a ghostly tentacle had grabbed hold of Azrael and dragged him into the hole.

"He's a mage. You can't kidnap a mage," Adrienne declared.

Babette pursed her lips. "We just saw it happen. At least I did. He didn't want to go. The tentacle didn't give him a choice."

"Tentacle?" A few gazes lingered on her, probably measuring her for a dragon-proof straitjacket.

"I'm telling you, I saw some transparent arm come out of nowhere and poof away with him," she insisted.

"Even if that's true, there is not much we can do about it now, is there? Besides, we don't need him anymore. Our original plan is still the best option, I think," stated Aunt Zahra.

"What plan?" asked Babette.

"The one where we trade an artifact for the hostage. We received a message when you were on your way here with the horseman," Zahra informed her.

"A message from who?" Babette was playing catch-up.

"The Shaitan. Apparently, we have one of the objects they're looking for in our possession," Zahra explained.

"No shit," Babette huffed. "Which one?"

"A ring that is going to be our ticket into getting

close to the Shaitan. Which is when we'll deploy the Rosie 2100." Aunt Yolanda practically rubbed her hands in supervillain glee.

Again, she was clueless. "Which is?"

"Portable heavy-duty vacuum system."

"You're kidding, right?" How epic they already had a weapon ready. "How did you know to develop them to fight genies?"

"We didn't. They were part of a maintenance line that didn't do very well. Apparently, humans prefer to push or pull around a vacuum, not wear them. They went on a stupidly good sale, and Elspeth insisted we buy them. We have dozens of them sitting in a warehouse."

Industrial vacuums, a way to confront the genies and beat them?

Babette fist pumped. "Heck yeah. Let's do this. Who wants to suck with me?"

When everyone in the room started chanting, "Suck. Suck. Suck," she had the urge to watch *Spaceballs*.

If only she had someone by her side to chill with while doing it.

Chapter Twenty

*Since he was on a roll, adding to his original
four vows: Find quieter allies.*

The dragons were wasting Azrael's time. He
knew better than to be drawn into their
drama.

He should have turned around the moment he
entered the room full of silvers and one demon.
Odd to find one here. He thought them extinct.
They'd been banished centuries before his birth and
were considered the biggest enemy to dragons until
the Iblis.

The arguing washed over him as he searched
the room once more for the golden king he'd heard
about. Not currently present, which only reinforced
his belief this was a small silver outpost, a family in
disfavor, now hoping to gain status by working with

a dragon mage of his stature. They were going to get eaten if they didn't stop bombarding him with questions and providing little to no answers.

He was just readying himself to scare the silver in front of him when he was literally dragged from their presence. No chance to cast a protective spell. Not a moment to even take in a proper breath before a tentacle thrust out of nowhere and seized him.

It dragged him into the nothingness with no way to escape. No way of even knowing if the tentacle had a destination or planned to drag him through that nothing space forever.

Before he could devise a plan of attack, he was thrust back into the world. Tossed really. He only barely kept his feet, quickly scanning the environ— a room he'd never seen before with only one familiar thing. The woman he'd been trying to find.

Shock gripped him. "Daphne?" Surely this was a trick. A spell. The Shaitan playing games with him.

"Azrael!" she squealed his name. "How did you get here?" Then added, "Who cares? You're here. That's all that matters. It's like my wish came true." She threw herself at him, and he caught her, his arms wrapping around her, feeling her solidness. Reacting to her presence.

It really was his Daphne. But how? How had he found her? Or had she found him?

His mind mulled over the situation and her words. Focused on one in particular. "You wished for me?"

"Yeah." She rubbed her face into his chest. "Dorky, I know. You've got better things to do than rescue me."

He lifted her chin so he could meet her gaze. "Rescuing you has been the only thing on my mind since you were captured."

"Really?" Her lips held a soft tilt.

How could she doubt it? "I even agreed to ally myself with the silvers to find you. But it turns out you found me."

"Not me. I've been locked in this room." She grimaced.

"You are unharmed?" He released her long enough to finally check.

"They didn't do anything to me. Yet."

"I won't let them hurt you." A vehement promise. "Now, I need to ask you something." He rubbed his thumb over the faint mark left by the glass shard when the Shaitan bottle broke. "How many wishes have you asked and been granted?"

A frown creased her brow. "I don't understand."

But he had a slight inkling. "You were the last one to touch the bottle before it shattered and released the genie."

"And?"

"It's a strange trait of the Shaitan. If you save

them or do them a favor, they owe you three wishes."

She blinked at him. "When did I save a genie?"

"When you broke the bottle?"

"You mean dropped it, because I didn't plan to break it." Her lips pursed.

"The vow is bound to action, not intent. You freed the Shaitan, which means you get three wishes. You used one to bring me here." Which had probably drained the monster of magic, given the complexity of the task, but it had managed to do it. Lucky for Daphne. A wisher who asked for the impossible usually ended up dying. The magic didn't like the greedy ones.

"This is like Aladdin when he rubs the lamp!"

"Aladdin was a traitor working with the enemy. You mean to tell me his story survived?"

"It even got turned into some movies." She shrugged. "And that's not important. Wishes. How do I know how many I have left?"

"You don't recall how many wishes you've made?"

She shook her head.

"If we're in luck, you'll have at least one left."

"I should wish for the bad guys to go away."

He shook his head. "If it were so simple, we would have done it ourselves. You cannot wish them dead. Nor for them to banish themselves. Anything that would be construed direct harm nulls the wish and could rebound on the person asking."

She blinked. "Did a lawyer make the rules? That seems rather precise and confining."

"Wishes have to be bound by possibility. Magic can't do everything. But in this instance, maybe it can spare your life. I want you to wish yourself out of here. Wish yourself somewhere safe."

"Not without you," she declared.

Chapter Twenty-One

The poster on the wall said it best; I would do anything for love.

Azrael shook his head. "I need to stay."

He couldn't be serious. Daphne stared at him. "I am not leaving you."

"You can and will. I want you far from here when I engage the Shaitan in battle."

"You can't fight two of them," she exclaimed.

"One of them should be weakened by the wish."

"If it's weak, then I probably can't ask it for another right away."

His lips pursed. "I want you safe."

"We don't even know if I still have a wish. What if I ask and nothing happens?"

"Then I'll find another way to make sure you're safe."

"And what about you?"

"I'm not important."

He had an answer for everything. It just wasn't the right one. "You're going to sacrifice yourself."

"I've lived long."

"You can't die." She shook her head. "That's what I'll wish for."

"Don't be foolish. Save yourself."

"I'd rather save us both."

"Beautiful, stubborn, why must you make this so hard?" he growled, dragging her close.

"Because this isn't fair. I just found you." She leaned her head on his chest and, knowing he might be close to dying, whispered, "I think I might be in love with you."

"Only might?" he teased as he stroked her hair. He tilted her chin and dropped a light kiss on her lips. "If I had a wish, it would be that we had more time together."

Despite circumstances, his statement might have led to sexy time, but the door slammed open, startling them apart.

Mr. Smoky appeared and said with a clear sneer, "If we could be nauseous, we'd be puking."

"Did someone ask for a plague?" Mr. Smoky's friend entered, only half formed and barely holding it together.

"Soon. First, we shall free ourselves. And you shall help us."

"You want my aid?" Azrael shifted to stand in front of Daphne. "Then release her."

"We think not. She is valuable to you, therefore useful to us." The weakened Shaitan wound around Mr. Smoky, parts of them merging. As if they shared strength.

"I know she has a wish left," he stated.

"And still too many of us left to be found," declared the moving shapes.

Their undulating nature made her nauseous. "I won't use my wishes to help you."

"Will you use them to help your lover?" The Shaitan flowed deeper into the room, the tendrils of smoke reaching for Azrael's legs.

He hadn't pulled his stave, yet. Nor did she get the tickly feeling when he was doing magic.

The smoke suddenly whipped around his legs, tightening and yanking, throwing him off balance. He hit the floor hard.

She threw herself into the smoke, hoping to break its hold. "Don't you hurt him. Or I won't help you."

He groaned. "Daphne, you mustn't."

"Quiet." The Shaitan tried to slap a magical gag on Azrael, but he spat it off.

"I'd rather die than let any of your kind loose."

"Because they can't be killed," she muttered.

"There is nothing in this world that can harm us. Nor even contain us forever." It cackled, pleased with itself. Frustration mounted inside of her. If only they had a way to truly harm the Shaitan. But Azrael said she couldn't directly wish for it. Surely there was a way around that rule?

"You won't win," Azrael declared, having managed to free himself from the smoke. He finally pulled his stave.

The Shaitan split, and she noticed Mr. Friend had regained his stature by feeding off Mr. Smoky. Strong enough for a wish?

"You know what. I think it's time I used my last wish." She stood with her chin tilted and clenched her fists as she said, "I wish that, from this day forth, the stave that Azrael currently wields be known as the God Killer, the one weapon that can destroy any sentient being in this Earthly dimension."

Chapter Twenty-Two

Vow number seven: Never underestimate a
clever woman.

The Shaitan bellowed in rage, wanting to deny
the wish, but it couldn't refuse. Couldn't stop
the magic from acting. After all, it didn't directly
harm the caster. Nor was it even very taxing.

The wish was granted.

The wave of power gushing out of the Shaitan
proved intense, and for a moment, Azrael feared
she might have overreached. Yet the wording of the
wish was precise and restricted it to one weapon.
What she asked was possible, and the wish might
have even been helped along by the world itself,
which didn't approve of the intruding monsters.

The stave, currently folded in its smaller shape,
didn't appear any different, but he could feel it, the

throb of possibility, unlike the sickly feeling the Dracinore exuded. This was a weapon he could use. It slapped into his hand, and he smiled.

The Shaitan, weakened by the wish, barely moved when the bladed edge of his stave swiped across. It cried out in surprised pain, but he didn't listen. Whirling his weapon, he kept slashing the Shaitan over and over, the wounds not healing, not bleeding.

It didn't scream when it died. Only dissipated into nothing.

For a moment, he stood there. It had almost been too easy. But he'd done it. He could fight.

Tapping his stave on the floor, he eyed the other monster, who actually gaped.

"You killed us."

Before he could throw himself at it, the Shaitan was gone, sliding into a dimensional rip. Finally afraid.

Whereas he had hope.

Daphne threw herself at him. "You did it. He's gone."

"So it would appear." But would the Shaitan reassemble at one point and return? Vigilance would be required.

"Come." He snared her hand. "Let us leave this place."

Her smile warmed him, but not as much as he

planned to warm her when he got her back to his cave. But that wouldn't happen yet apparently.

"If you're looking for the bad guy, he's on the roof."

The woman who appeared in the doorway startled him, but he'd met her briefly earlier at the silvers' house. "You are Elspeth. The seer."

"This is Elsie?" Daphne repeated. "I've heard about you."

"Which is probably less creepy than the fact I've been seeing you in my visions." Elspeth cocked her head.

"You're right, that is creepy," Daphne agreed.

"Don't worry. I've already seen we'll become great friends. Luc is going to teach your man to barbecue," Elsie claimed, clasping her hands and beaming wide.

"I am well versed in cooking meat," he said.

"On a spit over a bed of coals." Elspeth rolled her eyes. "That is so BC. You need to get with the current times. Reduce those carbon emissions. Learn how to grill electric."

He glanced at Daphne. "Mayhap we should have let the Shaitan take this world."

"They still might if you don't get to the roof." Elspeth eyed the ceiling only a second before they heard some thumping and yelling.

"Stay here," he barked.

With the Shaitan beholden to Daphne gone, she

had no wishes. No way to save herself if things went wrong.

"I am not waiting here to see if you live or die. Let's go." She marched past him to a door that led to a hall. And more doors.

"Where are the windows? The stairs?" Because he knew they were up several levels.

"This way." She headed for the far end of the hall and opened the door with the bright red letters above it. She pointed before going through. "That means exit."

He memorized it and then took the stairs going up two at a time. The locks on the doors didn't take long to break. He flung open the door to the rooftop and confronted the strangest sight.

People walked around, wearing loud machines and holding out hoses to suction the smoky edges of the Shaitan. More people looked on and cheered.

For his part, the Shaitan appeared panicked, tugging and stretching his frame, but he was being sucked in five directions.

Zahra, wearing an elegant pantsuit and holding a little box, stood to the side and watched.

For a moment, it seemed as if they would succeed. That the Shaitan would be split apart and contained in their vacuuming systems.

He really wished it would work, but his magic didn't function that way. Not to mention it would have been too simple.

One of the contraptions sputtered and died, but they still had four functioning ones and only a little more smoke to go. Until two more shut off suddenly. It didn't take a seer to know what would happen next.

Azrael charged for the Shaitan, feeling the energy coalescing, building, getting ready to snap. He raised the stave, ready to throw it like a javelin. The only chance he had.

But his attention was distracted by a shadowy movement. A cloaked figure moved stealthily amongst them, the eyes peering from the hood familiar.

Maalik.

Here and not dead.

Why was Maalik here, after all this time, standing by the matriarch, his cloak drawn low over his features?

The Shaitan cackled, drawing his attention to the fight.

The spear left his hand a second too late. The last two vacuums died, and the canisters began to shake.

"Drop them!" he yelled.

The wearers grabbed at their harnesses and tugged. Only two got them off, but they all remained too close together. The snap as the five pieces burst free and joined together knocked everyone on their ass.

The Shaitan shot into the air, a chuckling morass that suddenly swooped.

Azrael knew it was heading for his stave. The only thing that could kill it. If the Shaitan took it…

Azrael ran.

He wouldn't make it in time.

Maalik reached the God Killer first and plucked it from the ground before twirling.

The Shaitan drew up, and hovered.

Maalik drew back his arm and fired. The stave wasn't built for his lithe frame. It was off just enough that the monster escaped being speared. The stave landed close to Azrael.

He dove for it, his fingers curling around the haft. He rolled and popped to his feet, expecting to see the enemy behind him.

Only he'd miscalculated. The Shaitan stood at the edge of the building, a swirling mass of smoke and man. The monster held Daphne, dangling her over the deadly open space. "Anyone moves and the female dies." The Shaitan shook her for emphasis.

"Put her down," Azrael demanded. He hefted his stave.

"Are you really going to use that?" The Shaitan shook Daphne, who didn't utter a sound, but her eyes were wide with terror.

The spear in his hand became heavy. The choice before him was clear. He couldn't destroy the Shaitan without killing Daphne.

"What do you want?" Zahra asked, providing a distraction.

"Isn't it obvious? What I came for. Give me the ring in that box and you can have the human."

Azrael knew better than to agree, but Daphne's life hung in the balance. "Hand it over."

"I can't," the silver matriarch stated.

"Hand it over now," he growled, whirling to glare.

"I can't because I don't have it. I lost it during the explosion."

He heard the inconvenient truth and barked with a bit of power, "Who has the vessel?" When no one replied, he scanned the crowd. Maalik didn't appear to be in it. And neither was the seal.

"What a shame. Without the ring, I have no use for the girl."

"Wait," Azrael shouted. There had to be something he could do. Some kind of bargain. He eyed the stave in his hand. God Killer. The miracle he'd waited three thousand years for.

"Will you trade the spear for love?" hissed the Shaitan, his smirk despicable. The choice untenable.

The spear in his hand had the weight of the world in it.

Three thousand years he'd waited to end the curse.

Three thousand to find happiness.

He tossed the stave to the ground.

He'd give anything to have her back.

"You know what. I don't think I want to trade." The Shaitan's smile widened, a second before he tossed Daphne from the building!

Chapter Twenty-Three

Wondering if her Tinker Bell Halloween costume
would have made a difference...

Daphne had a second only to realize she was
going to die. When she'd seen Azrael give up
his spear, choosing her over vengeance and saving
the world, she'd been filled with such love and joy.

And then that bastard genie dropped her. She
would have peed herself if she wasn't plummeting
so fast.

Then she could have sworn she saw a cat,
perched on the shoulder of some gigantic dude in a
cape, looking down at her. The cat winked.

Time seemed to stop. Something pulsed out of
the hovering genie. And then it exploded into
smoky chunks as Azrael dove through it, spear first,
shattering the Shaitan and plummeting after her.

She opened her mouth and finally screamed. It cut off when he grabbed her, twisted them, and jabbed the spear into the wall of the building. He held the quivering length one-handed, the other arm anchoring her.

She'd never felt safer.

She smiled. "You saved me."

"You saved me first."

She leaned her head against him. "I'd love to argue the point with you, but first I have to ask, how are we getting down?"

"Magic of course. The question is, do you want to stay and listen to them talk just for the sake of hearing themselves, or go somewhere quiet?"

"Can we go back to your cave?" she asked. "I feel safe there."

"Your wish is my command." He flicked the wrist with the spear, dislodging it and sending them plummeting. He whispered, "Sleep," and she was so grateful to not have to feel that awful empty place. She was ecstatic to open her eyes to see him. He held her in his arms as he carried her through that tunnel to the bath.

"I can walk, you know."

"Why walk when I can carry you?" was his rejoinder.

He also insisted on stripping her, tearing her clothes from her body. His mouth was hot on hers, his body heavy. The pleasure fast and intense.

She clung to him panting, crying out his name.

Coming again, when he hoarsely shouted hers.

When he finally carried her to bed—her bed, the one he'd moved from her apartment—he took his time pleasuring her again.

His lips wrung cries as he licked her between the legs. She sobbed with relief when he stretched her with his cock.

And sighed as he cradled her close and said, "Remember how you once asked me what I hoarded?"

"Yeah. You wouldn't tell me."

"Because it was strange. I hoarded spots I liked to sleep."

"You mean beds?"

"Not exactly."

She leaned back to eye him. "Why are you explaining this now?"

"Because I just realized they weren't what I really wanted."

"What do you want?" she asked, her voice low.

"You."

Only later did she ask, "Do you think it's over?"

"The Shaitan that got loose were destroyed."

"What about the other vessels?"

"We'll search until we find them. And now that we have a weapon, we will destroy them. I'm not taking chances. Not now that I've found you."

Turned out Daphne didn't need a wish to have her happily ever after.

Epilogue

The cave became their base of operation. During the day, they went topside, seeking out clues for locations of the remaining vessels. The ring had never been recovered, although Azrael had his suspicions given Maalik's brief appearance on the rooftop. Was his presence what drew Israfil? Azrael had seen his large friend in passing as he dove off the roof, and nothing since.

He shoved down the pang that they'd disappeared without a word. Let them choose their own path. Azrael didn't need their help. He had more allies than he needed to seek out the remaining seals. But rather than dash about in a disorganized fashion, the Golden King's advisors had an idea.

They started a museum. Put Azrael's clever Daphne in charge, which gave her the authority to buy and access treasures that might lead them to what they were looking for.

While Daphne put her brain to work, he learned the world. Or at least parts of it. He visited major cities and, in each one, dropped into a deep trance to memorize a spot. He needed to be able to move quickly. To act at a moment's notice. Because the danger was far from over. It bothered him Maalik might have stolen a seal. Why would he do that? Was he about to pull an Aladdin and align himself with the enemy?

And what did Jeebrelle play at, visiting with that silver female?

He did his best to forget those questions when he collected Daphne at the end of the day and brought them back to his cavern, where they spent their time naked. Writhing. Pleasuring.

In between the excellent sex, she'd been decorating. Modernizing and stocking the place with goods. Because, as his mate liked to tell him, "If the end of the world comes, there's no place I'd rather be than here with you."

He felt the same. If the door to his prison were to slam shut tomorrow, he didn't think he'd mind anymore. Because he'd found the thing he'd been missing all those years: Love.

~

IT WAS RAINING AGAIN. Babette felt compelled to go and stand in it. She couldn't have said why. She didn't even have Elspeth to blame. Her BFF had returned to her castle with her demon, claiming they needed peace and quiet—which was a bit of an oxymoron given how much noise those two made.

They'd saved the world for the moment. Although there was worry still about the five missing seals. Even if they'd made it impossible for the mega Iblis monster to appear, five bad genies could cause more than their fair share of trouble.

But that wasn't why she was in the garden waiting.

It wasn't sound or scent that drew her attention. Yet she knew the exact moment Jeebrelle arrived. She greeted her with a smile. "I was hoping you'd come back."

THE END of the world had been averted, and Maalik knew he should be more thankful that Azrael had found a way to save them. Yet Maalik couldn't help a feeling of dissatisfaction.

All that time locked away, and the era before fighting the Shaitan, to discover it only took a wish to give them a weakness.

It was a mark of shame and embarrassment. But not the reason why he'd stolen the ring.

Could a well phrased wish make things right?

Let me loose, and I will give you everything your heart desires.

But what if what he wanted wasn't what he needed?

DRAGON'S JINN– MAALIK LOST THE ONE HE LOVED AND WANTS A CHANCE TO MAKE IT RIGHT, BUT EVEN A POWERFUL JINN CAN'T FIX A BROKEN HEART. OR CAN SHE? HE'S GOT THREE WISHES TO FIND OUT.

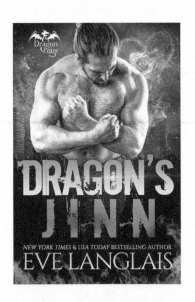

HAVE you read all the books in Dragon Point?

Dragon Mage

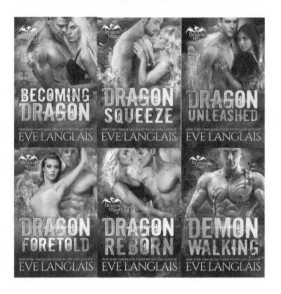